without a past

(a dakota steele fbi suspense thriller—book 3)

ava strong

Ava Strong

Bestselling author Ava Strong is author of the REMI LAURENT mystery series, comprising six books (and counting); of the ILSE BECK mystery series, comprising seven books (and counting); of the STELLA FALL psychological suspense thriller series, comprising six books (and counting); and of the DAKOTA STEELE FBI suspense thriller series, comprising five books (and counting).

An avid reader and lifelong fan of the mystery and thriller genres, Ava loves to hear from you, so please feel free to visit www.avastrongauthor.com to learn more and stay in touch.

BOOKS BY AVA STRONG

REMI LAURENT FBI SUSPENSE THRILLER
THE DEATH CODE (Book #1)
THE MURDER CODE (Book #2)
THE MALICE CODE (Book #3)
THE VENGEANCE CODE (Book #4)
THE DECEPTION CODE (Book #5)
THE SEDUCTION CODE (Book #6)

ILSE BECK FBI SUSPENSE THRILLER
NOT LIKE US (Book #1)
NOT LIKE HE SEEMED (Book #2)
NOT LIKE YESTERDAY (Book #3)
NOT LIKE THIS (Book #4)
NOT LIKE SHE THOUGHT (Book #5)
NOT LIKE BEFORE (Book #6)
NOT LIKE NORMAL (Book #7)

STELLA FALL PSYCHOLOGICAL SUSPENSE THRILLER
HIS OTHER WIFE (Book #1)
HIS OTHER LIE (Book #2)
HIS OTHER SECRET (Book #3)
HIS OTHER MISTRESS (Book #4)
HIS OTHER LIFE (Book #5)
HIS OTHER TRUTH (Book #6)

DAKOTA STEELE FBI SUSPENSE THRILLER
WITHOUT MERCY (Book #1)
WITHOUT REMORSE (Book #2)
WITHOUT A PAST (Book #3)
WITHOUT PITY (Book #4)
WITHOUT HOPE (Book #5)

PROLOGUE

Billie winced, rubbing at her sore leg where she'd bumped against the metal shelf. She carefully adjusted the stack of trash can lids she'd nearly toppled, grimacing against the scraping sound of metal. More than one customer had complained about the friction marks along the bottom of the containers upon purchase. She'd relayed this to the higher-ups. But did managers listen to shelf-stockers? No-siree.

She shook her head, trying to keep positive as she reset the shelf and then continued in her haste towards the back of the store.

"Ha! What happened to you, Billie?" a voice called from aisle six.

She adopted a sufficiently sheepish grin, tugging at one of her dark braids, her fingers scraping a red and blue bead woven into her hair. "Oh," she said, "Just a little accident. Spilled some of the ketchups." She glanced ruefully down at her stained, blue uniform. Her nametag was also covered in the red stain which went from her collar down to her ribs.

"Ha!" laughed Jeremy, another employee. An easy-going, kind man who often stole packs of chips when the managers weren't looking. "You look like you're in a slasher movie!"

She snorted, but continued on, her feet squeaking against the freshly mopped tiled floor. She'd been the one to mop it, early in the morning when she'd reported to the large shopping center for work.

But she didn't mind the odd jobs, or small indignities.

Her own mother had worked two jobs just to support the rest of them. And now Billie was paying her way through grad school.

She smiled at the memory of her mother when she'd announced her acceptance into the prestigious university.

Now, though...

Trash can lids and ketchup stains.

Such was life, she supposed. She sighed faintly, moving towards the supply closet in the back hall past the employee bathroom.

"It isn't break time yet!" a voice called after her from behind a counter near the information kiosk.

She couldn't see her manager, but she recognized Demi's voice well enough. Billie rolled her eyes, pushing one of her braids back behind an ear before calling out. "Thanks—just getting a clean uniform!"

"Hurry up—need to re-stack the display shelf. The chips fell."

"Of course they fell," Billie muttered beneath her breath. She'd told Demi they would fall. Out loud, though, she said, "Be right there!"

She reached the supply closet. The single light bulb above the door was sparking and flickering. She frowned. Maintenance had a work order for the bulb but were running behind due to the new expansion in the garden wares section of the store.

Billie, tugged faintly at her shirt, trying to separate the red stain from her skin. She twisted the handle to the supply closet, in the dark, flickering section of the back hall. The faint scent of bathroom powder kegs and cleaning supplies lingered on the air. Her fingers grazed the cold metal of the door handle. She shouldered the thin, flimsy wooden door inward and stepped into the large supply closet.

As she did, she heard the faint sound of whistling.

A janitor was in the back, fiddling with some of the window-cleaners.

"Hey Carl!" she called.

He raised a gloved hand, giving a brief little wave.

She turned away from the janitor, glancing at the nearest shelf. She wrinkled her nose. "Huh. All the mediums are taken I see."

Carl didn't reply. She heard the clink of glass and sloshing of liquids as he continued to work with the bottles.

She fingered at the blue material of one of the uniforms. XXL. It would hardly compliment her figure. She sighed, shifting through the pile of outfits, thumbing at the tags, and looking for a medium.

As she did, Carl brushed past her.

"Sorry," he muttered in a muted, almost muffled voice.

"No prob," she said, sighing and deciding she might as well go with one of the large shirts.

The janitor brushed past her, reached the door but didn't leave. She heard a faint *click*.

She frowned, turning. Carl was still facing the door. About two feet away from her, his back to her... Except... Wrong skin tone.

This wasn't Carl... And what was that thin elastic band wrapped around the back of his head, creasing his skin like a wire in a bread pan.

"Umm... s-sorry, sir are you new? Can I help you?" she said, hesitantly, frowning at the janitor.

He'd taken one of the spray bottles... except... it didn't look quite like any cleaning solution she'd ever seen. It came in a sleek, stainless steel container, with a strange, black nozzle with multiple sections like some sort of security feature. The sections, she noted, had been twisted free.

"Sir... sir..." she said, starting to feel tremors up her spine. She swallowed now, forgetting completely about the uniform for a moment. She took a hesitant step back. "Did you look the door?" she said, her tone suddenly frightened.

He didn't look at her, still facing the door, his face only inches away, but concealed from her gaze. "Yes," he murmured.

And only then did he turn to look at her.

The blood left her face. Her heart thumped wildly. A man wearing a gas mask was staring right back at her. The mask had an air filter at his chin, dangling like some sort of odd protrusion. The glass itself was streaked and spattered as if from much use.

She thought, vaguely, she could glimpse two dark eyes behind the mask, but this may have just been her imagination.

She was stumbling back now, stammering, louder—her voice rising in volume. "Hey... Hey! HEY! Get out of my way!" she yelled. "What are you doing—what do you think—"

He held a gloved finger to his lips, emitting a strange, filtered shushing sound through his mask.

"Sorry about this," he whispered, his voice still muffled. Then, he raised the steel container, pointed it right at her, and began to spray.

She felt flecks of moisture on her cheek, along her arms. The spray poured from the nozzle, expanding in the air, and lingering before landing in small droplets along her body and arms.

"HELP!" she screamed now. "HELP!"

But he was still holding his finger to his lips, making a shushing sound.

She inhaled shakily, something suddenly stinging her throat. Only a second later did she think to hold her breath. She grabbed one of the uniforms from the rack, holding it in front of her face. Her eyes were stinging now too.

The man with the gas mask didn't react. Didn't move. He just watched her, his head partially tilting as if gazing upon some unusual specimen.

Only one door.

Her eyes stung, watering now. Her throat felt as if it were tightening.

She tried to bolt towards the door, shoulder lowered, still screaming. But her legs wouldn't move the same way they had before.

She took two steps, then stumbled. Tried to put weight on her other leg, then fell completely.

She hit the ground with a painful gasp and tried to rise.

But even this was too much. Her arms were too weak. Her throat was on fire. It was difficult to see now, with tears streaming down her cheeks. Her fingers uncurled from where they clutched at the soft fabric of the blue employee shirt.

She felt the shadow of the figure at the door shift. He didn't come near her, preferring it seemed to watch his work from a distance.

He didn't look away either. Those dead eyes behind that streaked glass just watched her. If anything... he looked amused.

"H-help," she tried to cry out.

But he didn't move. Didn't touch her. Didn't try to help. In parting, he pointed his spray bottle at her, giggled in a muffled sort of way. And gave her a final little spritz of the liquid, like a child splashing a parent in a swimming pool. As if it were just a harmless, mischievous gesture.

But then her vision vanished as the stinging intensified. As her mind shut down, she heard the door unlock. Heard the sound of footsteps.

And then rapid footfalls. A shout—Demi's voice. Her manager.

At least someone had heard Billie's screams.

CHAPTER ONE

Dakota Steele's father answered the phone *finally*.

She glared at her device, staring at the logged calls. Four outgoing... he hadn't answered in nearly two days. But then, this morning...

"H-hello?"

She couldn't help herself. A lump formed in her throat as she listened to her father's rasping voice, stained with cigarettes but refusing to go quiet regardless.

"H-hey, Dad?" she said, her own voice unsteady.

"Dakota?" he said, his voice shaking. "Tastee, is that you?"

She wrinkled her nose. Tastee had been a nickname Coach Little had given her in her fighting days. A combination of her first and last name, suggesting—somewhat dramatically—that she had a taste for blood.

Coming from her father, it didn't land the same way. "Yeah... hey... hey Pop. You got a minute?"

"Ummm... Can... can I call you back in a couple minutes?"

Then, before she could reply, he hung up.

She went still. Staring at her phone... glaring. "Well then," she muttered slowly. Normally, Dakota prided herself on keeping her emotions in check. She liked being honest with herself—and with others—about her thoughts. But she also liked a sense of decorum. Appearances mattered.

But now... her father hanging up. They hadn't spoken—not really in... ten years? More? She couldn't say exactly. And the moment she reached him, he put her on hold.

Typical.

What more did she have to do? Send him a gift basket?

The previous day, she'd left two voicemails... but of course, the man wasn't interested.

She sighed in frustration, gripping her phone like a lifeline while standing in her apartment next to the small row of purple, Friend's Princess orchids she had been cultivating near the north-facing window of her new place. Ever since she'd left Rapid City, moving back to Quantico to return to her position with the BAU, the one piece of home she'd managed to maintain were these gorgeous purple flowers.

But now even the orchids weren't lifting her foul mood. Normally, Dakota wasn't one given to emoting. Certainly not in public. Appearances mattered. But in the privacy of her own apartment, it was sometimes difficult not to give voice to her frustrations.

"Call any time, dear," she muttered beneath her breath. "Would love to chat. In fact, I love you so much."

Then in a high-pitched voice, she replied. "Oh, thank you Daddy. You're so kind. I love you too. Thank you for not shutting down two decades ago and completely abandoning me."

"No, no," she said, putting on a fake, deeper voice. "I would *never* do that. I lost one daughter already. Why would I want to lose another out of sheer neglect?"

Dakota snipped back one of the drooping orchid flowers, lowering it into a small glass dish where she dried out the petals in the hope of using them as bookmarks, following a craft she'd seen on social media. Dakota hadn't grown up in a family that had cared about things like flowers or bookmarks.

The tattoos she had were testament to her earlier life, during her fighting days. The sleeve tattoo on her left forearm was of a dove being mauled by snake. That one had been the tasteful suggestion of an ex-boyfriend. The cartoon mouse on her other arm been a decision made in a drunken stupor. And the big skull and crossbones, like from a pirate's flag, just inside the wrist, had been a surprise—she still couldn't remember getting it.

Her tattoos were of a bygone area. While fighting, most of the athletes had been covered in the ink. But now, working for the BAU, she often regretted getting them. When out and about, she wore long sleeves, or turtlenecks to cover the tattoos. To hide them.

Appearances always mattered, regardless of what others said. She'd learned this in fighting, and learned this at the FBI. Her sea-gray eyes, and single-lumpy ear from her fighting days often attracted attention of a certain sort. She preferred to wear her hair neat and cut shoulder-length. All of it perfectly uniform, like a longer bowl cut. She was still passably attractive save a faint scar along the underside of her cheek which had never properly healed.

Now, her fingers flicked through this hair as she glanced back at her phone, scowling.

Her information request from the BAU was still pending. And so the only path forward she could think of where the serial killer known as The Watcher was concerned was to wait for Supervising Agent Carter to allow her access to files that the previous supervising agent had locked under suspicious circumstances. The Watcher was a notorious murderer, named for the third eye he painted in blood on his victims' foreheads. A few months ago, Dakota had been given a chance to catch the killer, but she'd made the wrong call.

He'd escaped.

A woman had died.

And now, once again, she was determined to hunt him down.

But she wasn't *just* requesting information on The Watcher.

No... she'd also asked for information on her sister's case as well. Two cases from her past. One from three months ago, the other from decades ago.

Dakota's eyes narrowed as she thought of her baby sister's cherubic features. She spotted the bloody backpack left on the side of the road. The only piece of evidence left when her sister had vanished nearly two decades ago.

The disappearance of Carol—named after North Carolina—was enough to break their family. Her father had stopped parenting Dakota. He'd turned into a shell of himself.

For twenty years now, his life's work had been to gather information about his daughter's disappearance. He kept it all in a thick red binder while he slept, next to the side of his bed.

Coach Casper Little, Dakota's only remaining friend in Rapid City, had occasionally given updates about her father.

But since then, her old man had moved.

She hadn't even known her childhood house had been demolished.

Feelings of neglect, of frustration, of loneliness swished through her as she glared at her phone, waiting for her old man to return the call. But he didn't... as the time ticked by, there was simply no return call.

She wondered if perhaps she ought to call him again...

But no... No, clearly he didn't want to talk.

She felt a lance of pain. A sharp jab of emotional agony somewhere in the vicinity of her stomach. She'd often experienced a strange emptiness when it came to her father.

She'd never blame another person for her own shortcomings... but sometimes she wondered if it might have been easier to quit drinking all those years if not for her old man's attitude towards her.

Still... she'd managed to stay sober for nearly a month now.

As the time stretched on, and the digital clock on her glowing blue screen continued to tick by, there were no further calls.

She held her phone, cradling it, feeling that anxiety, that loneliness, that bitterness in her stomach growing larger... larger... like flames stoked with fuel.

And then...

A text.

Her heart jumped.

But no—not her father.

She frowned. The frown didn't last *too* long though.

A mixture of emotions now. Equal parts disappointed, furious at her old man, but also... a sudden sense of bashful delight.

Agent Mark Bonet had texted her. They weren't *dating*. Not really. But... but she knew they found each other *interesting*. Bonet—a techie at the FBI—had been a division one linebacker. With her own background in competitive sports, they'd hit it off.

The text message was short but sweet.

Coffee this weekend?

They were still in the feeling out stage. But she couldn't hold back a smile now as she texted back. *Sure. What time?*

She hesitated before sending it, not wanting to appear *too* eager. But then, after a sufficient wait, she pressed send.

Still no call from her dad.

Part of her wanted to fling her phone across the room. "Damn it..." she muttered beneath her breath. She swallowed, feeling a strange... *urge* coming back that she was so familiar with.

She inhaled shakily, feeling that rising desire to go find the nearest gas-station or liquor store and pick, off the cheap rack, some of her favorites.

She could practically feel the way it would taste if—

The phone began to ring.

Thank God. She quickly lifted it. "Hello?"

"Agent Steele?" came a clipped voice.

Dakota's heart sunk again. Not her father, but rather Supervising Agent Carter. Dakota could picture the agent with her short-cut, pale hair and dark skin sitting behind a walnut desk beneath *far* too many security cameras. Dakota would never gossip about colleagues, and she certainly wouldn't accuse Carter of being paranoid to her face.

But the last time she'd been in the woman's office, the walnut desk had been moved in case of sniper fire.

It didn't help things between them that Agent Carter seemed to deeply dislike Dakota.

"Umm, hello, Agent Carter," Dakota said quickly, trying to manage her emotions again and returning to her usual, concise way of speaking.

"Where are you now?" Carter asked.

"Home, ma'am."

"Well come into the office now."

Dakota swallowed. "Is this... about my information request?"

"What request?"

"I—I sent them a couple days ag—"

"Haven't checked my emails from subordinates yet. Information can wait. We have a case. Hurry up—we're wasting time."

And then Agent Carter hung up.

Dakota puffed air slowly, frowning at her phone. Still no call back from her father. Maybe he was busy changing numbers or blocking her caller-ID. There was no shortage to the irritation she now felt towards her old man.

But on the other hand, though the conversation hadn't been friendly, Dakota could feel a slow sense of relief.

The one thing, the one high, the one buzz that hit the spot even better than a drink...

Was the adrenaline rush of the hunt.

Dakota didn't just chase bad guys for noble reasons.

She did it for the thrill. For the rush.

And by the sound of things, another opportunity had just come center stage.

Carefully checking her pockets for keys and wallet and ID, she hastened towards the door to grab her long-sleeved turtleneck draped over a chair and to pick up her shoulder holster.

As she hurried out the apartment door, she almost forgot her call to her father again.

Almost...

But a small, background part of her subconscious couldn't help but build resentment. Her old man's choices were beyond her control. And while Agent Carter wasn't a friend, Dakota knew the better her job performance, the easier to make information requests.

With or without her father. With or without Carter, Dakota was determined to go back through the case from three months ago... the case she'd failed that had led to the death of a young woman.

But she was also determined to look into her sister's disappearance.

It was only a matter of time.

The door to her apartment slammed shut behind her. The sound of her footsteps, hastening towards the stairs, accompanied the faint jingle of her keys as she slipped them into her pocket.

CHAPTER TWO

Dakota stepped into Agent Carter's office, her eyes roaming the room. She spotted three separate security cameras easily visible, and more than one hidden in the bookshelf at the far wall. The windows were covered in dark drapes, preventing line of sight from the parking structure across the street.

And again, Agent Carter's large desk had been moved.

Dakota could see the imprint in the floor where the desk had settled a few days ago. But now, it was on the other side of the room, facing the door.

"Sorry I'm late," Dakota said more as a formality than anything. She doubted Carter would care to cut her any slack. And she doubted the second figure in the room would care to give her any grief.

The short-haired, middle-aged woman behind the desk glared over a bronze statue of a bull. Her hands were folded neatly in front of her on a computer mat.

The giant of a man, Agent Marcus Clement, threatened the existence of the small chair he reclined in. The dark, handsome man was smiling at her, flashing perfectly maintained, perfectly white teeth. He wore a comic book shirt visible just beneath his suit jacket and tie. She couldn't make out the particular characters on his shirt this time, but the body-builder had a penchant for nerds and geeks who turned into gods. She didn't know comic books particularly well, but she never talked down on them when Marcus was around.

The one thing Marcus enjoyed more than lifting weights at the gym, was memorizing words and sharing his pet-favorites with the people he most liked. To Marcus, a newly discovered word was the same as a house-warming gift or a birthday surprise.

So it wasn't unusual that instead of greeting her by name, he said, "Schadenfreude."

She glanced at him, back at Carter who was still frowning, then at Marcus again. "Dunno," she said.

"Guess," he said cheerfully.

"A type of ice cream?"

"No, no," he replied. "More like delight in someone's suffering."

Dakota nodded. "Seems appropriate," she murmured, but quickly returned her attention to Carter.

Agent Carter very much liked Marcus. So this sort of preamble was only met with a good-natured nod. But Carter disliked Dakota, so any time Dakota spoke it was met with a glare.

Now, the supervising agent was gesturing towards one of the seats next to Marcus. "Come along," she was saying. "Sit, sit. We don't have all day, Agent Steele."

Marcus winced apologetically and conspicuously turned to face their supervising agent.

The two of them went quiet now, watching Carter.

She cleared her throat. "Glad to have you both here." This time, though, her look of frustration didn't linger *so* long on Dakota. They had solved the last case, after all. Dakota had to hope this was earning her *some* level of good graces.

"Now," Carter was saying, "The case in question is in Arizona. So I hope you two pack some sunscreen. Two victims so far."

"And what connects them as victims?" Marcus said.

Agent Carter glanced at her computer screen, her features illuminated by a low, blue light.

"The first woman," Carter said slowly, "was killed by carbon monoxide poisoning."

Dakota leaned in now, still keeping her posture professional, but interested. "And how do we know it was murder?"

"According to the first responders, an outboard heater was rigged to spew fumes into the garage. The job was sloppy, but intentional. Also," Carter looked over her steepled hands, "the door camera was stolen."

"What about the victim's phone?" Marcus said.

"Sonja Pierce was found in her garage, dead, with no phone, and no house keys. The doors were locked. House keys were found inside."

"Is it possible she locked herself in the garage?" said Dakota.

"The initial findings suggested that was a possibility. But a coroner's report came back yesterday, and it indicated that prior to the carbon monoxide, Ms. Pierce ingested some type of tranquilizer."

"So the killer drugged her, then killed her?"

"So it would seem." Carter tapped a finger against her keyboard, and moved on to another case file, judging by the sudden shift in lighting against her face from the glowing screen. She frowned, and said, "Our second victim is Billie Childs. She was working at a supermarket when she was trapped in a supply closet and killed."

"Same MO?"

"Yes, Clement, she was attacked with a tranq combined with

11

something else. The coroner says it looks like mustard gas."

Dakota wrinkled her nose, scowling. "Like weaponized gas?"

Carter nodded. "According to our lab it's as if the killer made it himself."

Dakota leaned back.

"Did anyone see anything at either location?" said Marcus.

"Nothing yet. But the employees at the supermarket haven't been questioned yet. The body was only found this morning. The toxicology report wasn't confirmed until a couple of hours ago. And the only reason we were able to run it so fast was by matching it against results from the last murder."

"So when was Ms. Pierce killed?"

"Tuesday, two days ago."

Marcus was frowning, pushing to his feet now, and gently pressing a hand against Dakota's shoulder as if prompting her to rise as well. "Sounds like we need to get going," Marcus said. "Do we have flights booked?"

Carter nodded once. "Flights are handled. We already have a car lined up to meet you at the airport. And remember sunscreen. Arizona can be sweltering this time of year."

Dakota brushed at her long suit sleeves, shifting uncomfortably. In the warm weather, it would be difficult to wear turtlenecks without drawing attention. But she could just about feel where the edge of her collar pressed to her throat, obscuring the tail of the dragon tattoo she had gotten years ago.

Sacrifices had to be made to maintain an appropriate appearance.

"And agents," said Carter, firmly, "we have DEA, ATF, and Homeland Security all looking over our shoulders on this one. The chemicals being used don't look like they are geared towards a massive terror attack, yet. But I wouldn't rule it out." She leaned forward. "We don't want to find out what happens if this guy starts getting out of control. Understand?" Her voice struck like a gavel. "Bring him in. Now."

And with those chilling words, Marcus turned, leading Dakota back out the door, and away from the stern frown of Agent Carter.

CHAPTER THREE

He didn't think of himself as anything less than brilliant.

A genius.

And who could question him?

He smirked to himself, as he moved about inside the small trailer which he had parked at the foot of a sand dune; the heat whisked through his small home, carrying grains of sand through the window. He inhaled slowly, taking in the warm scent of the desert.

No towns for miles. No cops for miles either.

Glass bottles shifted—a flask was dumped into a large beaker over a Bunsen burner.

He watched as the bubbles swirled, and the color of the liquid changed.

He nodded slowly to himself. The percolation had to be timed. The gas distribution would have to be measured. Everything about this was art.

Not just science. Chemicals were far more than science. They were the paints, but the final product was the portrait. And he was the master artist.

He nodded to himself as he moved quickly through the small space.

If anyone did stumble upon his trailer in the desert, no doubt they would suspect they had found some sort of cook lab. A meth factory.

But he had never consumed dopamine-dumpers. He made his own version of mind altering concoctions. But for him, the pleasure was in trying out his creations on others.

He didn't partake.

There were too many horror stories about what could happen to a mind like his if altered chemically. And the world needed his mind. Everyone needed his mind.

He felt a flash of rage as he considered this last part. As he considered just how poorly he had been treated.

He frowned to himself, turning up the heat a few notches. He had a small, temperature gauge attached to the side of the beaker with a non-active adhesive—he continued to watch the bubbles, and watched the thermometer.

As he waited, he turned slowly, adjusting the goggles over his eyes.

He peered out, staring into the desert, his gaze trailing over the sand dunes.

Sometimes, ATV riders would come through. But mostly, the place was abandoned.

Twice now, he had made a statement. Twice now, he had managed to communicate his message.

He was painting in bold strokes. But there were subtleties ahead too. It all made sense to him. When da Vinci had painted the Mona Lisa, he hadn't taken input from his lessers. Art by committee wasn't art at all. Which was why he'd been forced to come out here. The last place he had created hadn't appreciated his particular skillset. Hadn't appreciated the savant in their midst.

Now, he glanced back, and cursed.

Faint foam bubbles were spilling over the side of the beaker. Where the bubbles landed on the safety counter, sizzling burn marks were left in the lacquered wood.

A couple of strands of the liquid also spilled down the cabinet in the center of his recreational vehicle. Where the liquid touched wood, it immediately began to hiss and steam, corroding and eating.

He hastily adjusted the temperature, keeping his gloves as far from any of the spillage as possible.

He breathed slowly, shakily. He couldn't allow himself to get distracted. He had only just started.

The real work was about to come. And he had so many more ideas. Messages. Gifts he would present them with. They wouldn't be able to resist.

CHAPTER FOUR

Dakota stretched, rubbing at her neck and wincing as she pushed out of the taxi which had taken them from the airport. The heat instantly assaulted her. She winced, shifting uncomfortably in her chosen long-sleeve shirt.

"I guess Carter made a mistake with scheduling," Marcus said as he followed out the back of the taxi, having retrieved his credit card from the driver.

The yellow vehicle turned away from the parking lot, drove across two sets of painted white lines, and moved back towards the main highway.

Dakota watched it leave, curious, but then shot a look back towards her partner. "How do you mean?"

"She said someone was going to pick us up."

"Maybe she canceled it," Dakota muttered, turning to glance towards the large supermarket on the other side of a pedestrian walkway.

"Why would she cancel it?"

"Because she hates my guts." Dakota hefted her small briefcase, and began moving towards the large shopping center.

Marcus followed. Dakota walked with stiff, rapid strides; Marcus was able to move lazily, long legs covering twice the distance with half the effort. "She does not hate you," Marcus said.

"She does. You can't be serious."

"She's just hard to get used to sometimes. I'm sure, if you get to know her, she'll be–"

"I don't want to get to know her, Marcus. I want to be allowed to do my job." Dakota was often able to keep her emotions in check. But she was also known among her colleagues for telling the truth. The full truth. Which excluded normal omissions and obfuscations. She didn't see the point in misleading others.

Marcus was also honest. But he came with a bedside manner and now he was saying, "I wouldn't be too harsh. She's new, just like you."

Dakota shot her partner a look as the two of them crossed over the white lines, moving through the sliding glass doors.

"You know what I mean," he said quickly. "I'm not saying you're new to the FBI. Just saying you're back for the first time. And she recently was hired for her position too. It's a feeling-out process."

"And I'm feeling resentment and a big dose of contempt," Dakota muttered.

But then, she went quiet, straightening

Two police officers were standing in front of the large glass doors inside an air-conditioned entry vestibule. They held up their hands, and one of the men said, "I'm afraid the store is closed for today."

But Marcus flashed his badge. The cops quickly lowered their hands.

The leading officer who was wearing a baggy uniform a size too large for him, said, "We have the manager still waiting in the back. She keeps asking how much longer."

Marcus nodded quickly. "How long has she been there?"

"Umm... Think she went home for a couple of hours, but we asked her to come back in time to speak with you. She's been by the sandwich shop for nearly two hours. We have another officer with her."

Dakota nodded. "And did we get statements from the other witnesses?"

"A few. But the only one who saw anything substantive is waiting for you guys." He jerked a thumb over his shoulder.

Dakota nodded curtly while Marcus flashed a smile and a thumbs up. The two of them moved through the sliding glass doors, between the cops.

It only took a second for Marcus, thanks to his high vantage point, to spot their witness.

Dakota saw her too. Tearing a piece of paper to shreds. The woman sat at a table in front of the sandwich shop, and another officer sat bored at another table, looking at her phone.

The witness continued to shred the paper into smaller and smaller pieces. She sent them scattering across the table, and watched as they fluttered with her rapid breaths.

Dakota shot Marcus a quick glance. "She looks nervous."

"One of her employees was killed," Marcus replied quietly. "I feel bad for her."

The two of them moved across the tiled floor which looked as if it had been recently mopped. The faint, satisfying squeak of her shoes against the tiles propelled Dakota towards their witness. The manager, waiting for questioning, looked up as they approached.

She bit her lip nervously. The woman had big, curly hair. Her eyes displayed eyelash extensions. She had a tasteful amount of makeup, but lipstick that was a shade too bright.

She wore a golden cross around her neck, and her long, paste-on fingernails kept tearing at the paper parchment.

As Dakota drew near, she realized it was a receipt.

She glanced at the shreds of paper, then up again.

Dakota, as often was the case, allowed Marcus to speak first. Her partner had a much better bedside manner

"Are you Demi White?" Marcus said, his voice pleasant, and soft.

The woman looked at the giant, swallowed, and nodded once.

Marcus adjusted his spectacles on his nose, and sniffed. "Pleasure to meet you. I'm Marcus Clement. This is Dakota Steele. Do you think we could ask you a few questions?"

Demi shifted uncomfortably in her chair. She shot a look towards the female officer who was watching them with renewed interest. "When can I go home?" Demi said.

"We'll ask you some things, and then you're free to go," Marcus said.

The woman sighed, but crossed her arms over an ample chest. She wore a dark, blue uniform with a folded collar. A golden name tag rested on one side of her large chest. "I can't imagine what I could possibly tell you," she said. "I already told the police."

"Yes, well, we were hoping we could get it firsthand."

Marcus slowly sat in a chair that was far too small for him. Dakota remained on her feet, shifting uncomfortably from one foot to the other.

Demi glanced between the two of them. She sniffed. "I didn't hear his voice. I didn't see his face. All I saw was a blur."

Marcus was nodding. "Tell me about this blur."

She fidgeted. "I heard noise from the supply closet. I went back to investigate. I thought maybe Billie was stuck. She was a good girl, but a bit more book smart than street smart if you know what I mean."

"What *do* you mean?"

The woman huffed, sending a few strands of the shredded receipt across the table. She said, "I mean, she was only working here to pay her way through school. She wasn't treating this like a career. I've been here for like six years," the woman said, importantly, straightening her posture. "You can tell the ones who are going to stick around. There's an attitude."

Marcus nodded. "So you mentioned you heard something. Could you describe what you heard?"

The woman bit her lip. Her long eyelashes fluttered. She swallowed slowly and said, "I didn't realize at first. But I think it was screaming. I

17

went back to check, and then I heard something. I couldn't tell you what. Maybe the sound of footsteps. The door opened, and a figure brushed past me. I didn't even see him. I was too busy staring into the closet."

Dakota winced. On the flight over, she'd seen pictures of the crime scene.

They hadn't been pretty; the chemicals used to kill the second victim had ruined her corpse.

"I see," Marcus said quietly. "And the figure who rushed past you— do you think you could describe him?"

"No. I already told the officers, I couldn't see him. I don't even know what he looked like. Besides... I—I felt funny breathing in the air from the room. It made me light-headed, so I retreated. But I lost sight of the man."

"Did you see his face?"

"I don't think so. I didn't see much. He brushed past me so quickly. I thought he was our janitor."

"Why did you think that?"

"He's the only person who regularly uses the supply closet. He was wearing one of our blue uniforms."

"But you didn't see his face?"

She paused, frowning. Then she shook her head. "I'm sorry. I didn't see anything. I reached the door, and saw Billie laying on the ground."

"Then what did you do?"

"I tried to wake her, then ran to get help. I called 911."

"Good choice," Dakota murmured; Marcus nodded sympathetically.

"I didn't know what to do. She was bleeding, and it was all so horrible. I didn't know if she had something like one of those horrible diseases you hear about from the news. I was worried about touching the blood, so I didn't get too close."

Marcus reached out, patting the table next to the woman's hand. "You made the right choice. If you had breathed in the air too long near her, it might have been you on the floor with her. Is there anything else you can tell us? Was there anyone here who disliked Ms. Childs?"

"Everyone liked her. We knew she wouldn't last long. But that wasn't personal. Like I said, there's a lot of temporary employees that come through."

Marcus gave the woman a quick nod of gratitude. He shot Dakota a look.

But she couldn't think of anything to add.

Dakota glanced around, eyes on the ceiling. There were cameras every now and then. "Did he show up on security footage?" she said. But this question was addressed to the policewoman at the table across from them.

The cop shook her head. "We checked. He avoided the cameras. Nothing picked him up."

Dakota looked back at Demi. "Are there cameras in that supply closet?"

"No. Some of the employees use it for a changing room. New harassment policies forbid cameras from being in there."

Dakota nodded, glancing back to Marcus.

She listened faintly as the tall man murmured gently once more, appeasing Demi, assuring her she'd done the right thing.

Dakota was no longer listening, though. She'd already reached a decision. They needed to visit the coroner—to figure out *exactly* what this man was doing to his victims.

If the killer had avoided detection, while killing a woman in the middle of the day, he wasn't lacking for courage—the problem with the bold types was that often they would want the world to recognize their accomplishments. There was often a narcissism attached to killers like this and if this person could manipulate chemicals, using them to kill, she could only hope that he didn't try to target an entire store, or stadium.

But even one more death was too many.

He had killed on Tuesday. Then killed again today, Thursday. Which meant they didn't have much time to catch him before he continued his spree. The next step would have to be the coroner.

CHAPTER FIVE

The heat of Arizona was starting to get to her. Dakota shifted uncomfortably, tugging at the turtleneck she'd insisted on wearing. The coroner sat across from them, on the small terrace with garden furniture beneath a large umbrella.

The man was sipping a martini, wearing a lab coat.

Dakota sat in a metal chair across from him, frowning. Agent Clement kept glancing towards the metal door which led to the basement where the coroner's office resided.

But according to the man, he was on lunch break.

"Do you think we could take this inside?" Dakota said carefully, fanning at her face.

The old man lowered his martini with a smack of his lips, letting out a long sigh. He had a strange set of metal pliers jutting out of a white lapel pocket. A rusty hue stained the white cloth beneath the implement.

Dakota wrinkled her nose, trying not to stare at the thing. "Dr. Salenger," Marcus tried, "it's a bit warm out—what if we—"

But the old man waved a liver-spotted hand. "No, no. I'm on my break," he said for the second time in as many minutes. "Are you sure you don't want anything? My nephew runs the place." He gestured towards the small cocktail bar located above the coroner's office. The place was closed for the afternoon and wouldn't open until late in the evening according to signs on the door.

But the man sipping his martini had been given an exception by the other, dark-browed fellow behind the cash-register in the air-conditioned lounge.

The patio seating now served as the breakroom for the geriatric doctor.

Dakota sighed in resignation. She kept fanning at her face, adjusting her long turtleneck. Eventually, she wondered if she'd have to shed her long sleeves for something a bit more climate appropriate.

Now, her eyes darted from the rusty stain on the coroner's lapel to the tufts of gray chest hair jutting out past his collar. The man had spilled a bit of his beverage which had dripped down his chin and into his chest hair.

Dakota glanced up, wincing at the red and white umbrella above her, and more specifically at the glaring sun attempting to pierce through the fabric.

The dry air was also irritating Dakota.

One month sober—the longest she'd gone in a while.

But now... she swallowed in the heat, trying her best not to stare towards the many options lingering on the cocktail counter.

Sitting in the heat with the coroner wasn't the only irritation.

Her father still hadn't called back.

Agent Carter still hadn't approved the information request. She hadn't denied it, either. But Dakota was beginning to worry that *nothing* she did would earn the good graces of her new supervisor. Then again... solving this case couldn't hurt.

"So," Salenger said slowly, smacking his lips and leaning back in his metal chair. His white coat pressed through gaps in the back of the chair. "We have one victim who has died from some concoction similar to mustard gas. And another who's perished to carbon monoxide poisoning. That right?"

"Umm... Is it?" Clement asked.

"Oh... oh... Well, let me see." The man took another long sip, then placed his flat glass on the table and quickly fished out his phone. He frowned, muttering darkly as he tried to navigate his passcode. It took him a few tries, and each time, he'd glare deeper and scowl. Finally, he waved a hand over his shoulder.

"Romy, come here!"

The man behind the register lowered a towel and moved out onto the patio. "Yeah?"

"Phone—phone... please." The coroner waited impatiently as his nephew helped him enter his passcode. Then, the cocktail bar owner went back inside and Salenger turned to the two agents.

"Ah, yes—here we are. Right here." He grinned, his wizened cheeks curling up, his mouth twisting in a smile. "Beautiful. Absolutely stunning," he murmured. He turned the phone to show a picture of one of the victims that Dakota had seen on the plane.

She felt certain she would never *unsee* it.

"The megapixels," the old man was saying. "Three times as good as my last phone. My nephew recommended it. What do you think?"

"Very... very clear image," Marcus said nodding politely.

Dakota just pursed her lips, waiting impatiently in the sweltering heat.

"Right... well... Hmm... So yes, carbon monoxide and some

unknown gas—close to mustard gas. Not my area, but the lab seemed certain. So..." he lowered the phone. "What was it you wanted to know?"

"About the tranquilizer," Dakota interjected. "The one used in both victims."

"Right... hmm... Again—yes, again, this had to come back from the lab. Let me see." This time, thankfully, he managed to unlock his phone himself. He cycled through the images and then nodded, tapping a long finger against the glass of his phone. "Here we are," he declared. "Wonderful. Yes. Perfect. So... looks like..."

He paused, then nodded, every movement, every word seeming even slower than the one before to Dakota.

"Yes. It is a type of compound found among big game hunters... Or zoos."

"Zoos?" Dakota said.

"Yes. Where they keep animals so the public can—"

"I know what a zoo is, er, *sir*." She added this last part at a sharp glance from Clement. He sometimes served as her social conscience. She cleared her throat, trying her best not to clench a fist in frustration. "Is there anything we can do to locate the origin of it?"

"Well... this particular brew," he said slowly, wrinkling his nose as he studied his phone, "is even stronger than most... Tampered with."

"So this guy is making his own cocktails," Dakota said, realizing that alcohol was on her mind. She winced, shaking her head. "I mean... he's making his own recipes."

"Possibly. Very possibly."

Dakota sighed, leaning back, shrugging towards Marcus. "Did either of our victims work for a zoo, maybe?"

Marcus shook his head. "No... The first victim had a slew of jobs, including a fry-cook, an associate writing professor, a dishwasher, and something with dogs."

Dakota perked. "Dogs? Like a vet? They have tranqs too, don't they?"

"No—no," Marcus said. "She was a dog walker."

Dakota sighed, slumping back in her seat, wishing more than anything she could figure out a way to choke-out the sunshine. She'd made a career of kicking ass... Often she felt bad about it afterwards.

But now, in the heat, facing chemical vapors that could be carried on something as intangible as a breeze, she was beginning to feel out of her depth.

But the last two cases had gone well...

She had to remember this. To focus on it.

The last two cases had gone marvelously well.

So... she just had to solve this one also.

The coroner had finished his drink and was signaling his nephew for another one. Marcus shot Dakota a look, raising an eyebrow. She began to say something, but suddenly, her phone began to ring.

She glanced down, frowning.

An unknown number. But she recognized it.

Her father was calling back.

She felt her heart skip. She swallowed and held up a finger. "Umm, sorry. I gotta take this."

She quickly pushed out of her seat, the metal chair legs scraping against the patio floor. She hastened towards the entrance of the basement unit. She didn't enter, but once she was far enough away from the men on the patio, she ducked in the shadow of the unit, sheltering from the sun.

Sweaty, frustrated, and starting to feel her temper spark, she answered.

"Hey," she said. She hadn't meant to sound so unfriendly.

Her father's rasping voice replied. She still couldn't believe just how *old* he sounded. "Dakota?" he said. "Hey—sorry Tastee. I got in a bit of a fender-bender."

She froze, feeling some of her frustration deflating now to be replaced by guilt. The thoughts she'd been having towards her father had not been very kind ones. Then again, in the last couple of decades, these had been mostly par for the course.

"Shit. Are you okay?"

"Yes, yes, fine," he said. It sounded like it almost pained him to speak. "Got it sorted out. Had to get the car towed though. Anyway, I wouldn't have hit him if not for your call. But oh well."

She paused now, frowning. Was he blaming *her* for his accident?

She felt the thought niggling at her. She wanted to say something, but instead forced back a retort. She said, "Hey... I... Sorry to call out of the blue like that."

"Yeah," he said simply.

"But... I was wondering if you have a second."

"Okay."

He wasn't exactly giving her much to work with. She tried to keep her frustration in check, though. "I was hoping maybe you and I could chat about something... I... I don't know if you know but..."

"You're back in Rapid City. Little told me."

"Oh... Umm. No, actually. I was. But I'm in Virginia now. I actually... I work for the FBI." It was painful, like dragging nails across a chalkboard. But her father was the path forward. The only way to piece together what had happened to her sister after all these years.

She'd made up her mind a few days ago...

So why was it so damn hard to speak the words *now*?

"I see," he said slowly. "Huh. Alright. Yeah, Little mentioned you were some type of cop."

"Not a cop," she said testily. "You know what, that's not important. Just... I was wondering..." This was the hard part. "Is there a chance I could get a look at that red binder you keep?"

A pause. A swallowing sound. She could practically hear the frown in his voice. "Who told you about my binder?"

"Dad, I lived with you until I was a teenager. I *saw* the damn thing."

He didn't reply.

"Casper also mentioned you're still filling it."

"I do what I can," he said. "Which is more than I can say for some. I'm an old man... I do what I can."

Now, she couldn't hold back her retort. She shifted in frustration beneath the shelter of the basement entrance. She frowned now, trying to keep her voice low, and occasionally shooting glances back towards the patio. The faint murmur of voices suggested Marcus and Salenger were still in conversation.

"Are you implying I'm not doing what I can?" she said.

"Dunno. I don't even know you. Been what? Ten years?"

"Shit," she said, muttering now. "I knew I shouldn't have called." She wanted to yell at him. Wanted to lash out and hang up.

But she still needed those files. The case on her sister's disappearance had been dead for two decades. The only person who'd been keeping an eye on it had been her father.

The path through was with his help.

So she bit back an angry retort. Instead, trying to stay calm, she said, "Maybe I didn't help as much as I could. But I'm helping now. So can I get a look at that stuff, or not?"

"Help?" he said, still rasping. "Damn, kid. You ran away."

"I ran away? You chased me out! You weren't even there! You were either drinking or talking to your cop buddies or surfing the internet on some damn conspiracy theory!" She hadn't meant to start yelling. But she couldn't help herself. Her voice came loud and furious, summoned from somewhere deep within.

She could feel her skin prickling across the backs of her hands as they so often did before a fight. Before a drink.

"Whatever. Did you call me to yell at me?"

"No! I called you for some help! But I guess that's too much to ask, isn't it. Ha! I should've known better."

Her father hung up.

She glared at the phone now, seething. Part of her wanted to call him back just to get the last word... But what would be the point?

The voices on the patio had gone quiet now. She glared, jabbing her phone into her pocket. She marched away from the shelter, from the shade, stepping back out into the blistering sun.

"Time's up," she said to Marcus. "Can we go?"

The big man paused, watching her closely. "Are you alright?"

"Marcus... Please?"

The agent turned to the coroner who was busy with his second drink. "Thank you, Dr. Salenger. If anything else comes up, here's my card." The coroner nodded politely, but left the business card resting on the table, untouched.

Marcus let out a sigh then turned, moving towards Dakota, watching her closely.

She looked away. She didn't like being scrutinized.

Didn't like being under someone's microscope.

Her father wouldn't help. Of course not. He'd been a bum for a decade, he'd be a bum again...

She wasn't proud of these acidic thoughts, but they were hard to keep back, nearly impossible to keep at bay.

She waited as Agent Clement joined her, taking some respite in the shadow cast by his sheer girth.

"I'll call the taxi, shall I?"

"Hotel?" she said.

"Yes. We can settle in and then set up with internet. I think it's best..." he paused, glancing as if double-checking she didn't need his emotional support. But when she didn't bat an eye, he continued. "...if we check into zoos or big-game hunting or park rangers. Maybe there will be some connection with the tranquilizer."

"Perfect," Dakota said. She didn't like sounding like a sullen child. But it was hard to think of anything positive where her old man was concerned. He didn't know half the damage he caused. Didn't know what it was like to grow up in a home with a dead mother and an absent father.

Dakota tried her best not to feel sorry for herself.

There were worse things, she supposed.

Things that their two victims had experienced.

"Hotel," she said, in a softer voice. "Maybe... make sure it has air-conditioning. And a pool."

Marcus chuckled, nodding, lifting his phone and turning politely to allow Dakota her space to seethe.

CHAPTER SIX

He'd returned out of the desert, but could still feel grains of sand in the collar of his shirt. He swallowed briefly, peering over the backyard fence, his eyes peering through a dusty, streaked windshield.

Maintaining a vehicle, or even goggles, or anything in between, had never seemed like the most *important* use of his time.

His time was *very* valuable.

He'd once made as much as two hundred dollars *per hour.* He smiled at the memory, nodding to himself. But his expression became rather fixed in the front seat of his RV as he remembered how that particular job had ended.

His scowl morphed, but as the negative emotions began to rise, his attention was captured by a silhouette.

A figure ahead, moving across a window.

He swallowed, his eyes attentive, his heart pounding. He licked his lips faintly, softening the dry tissue. For that was what he was. Tissue and blood. Organs and muscles and sinew.

And so was she...

And yet such wonderfully *formed* tissue. He watched as her silhouette moved across the window. Watched as she paused and then moved back the other way.

This, he knew, was her bedroom. Below was the living room.

He'd stopped by before, scoping out the landscape.

Preparation was the most important part of creation.

He was an artist, and his muse continued to move in the safety of her apartment.

He swallowed again, wincing under the sun. Sooner or later he'd have to introduce himself... Tonight... tonight he'd do it. But not at her home... no—not this time. This was important. He'd wait for her to get in her car... follow... and then... He'd chosen the perfect spot.

He glanced into his backseat, smiling at the bottles in the steel containers. He'd created a new message. And she...

He glanced back at the window.

Was going to be his messenger.

CHAPTER SEVEN

"First a cocktail bar, now a swimming pool," Marcus murmured. "I'm starting to feel like I'm on vacation."

Dakota glanced over, across the sunchairs, raising an eyebrow. She felt a note of wry humor. "You look like you're going to a comic book convention."

Marcus blinked at her from behind his spectacles. He'd taken his suit jacket off, resting it neatly on the chair at his side.

Though they were sitting in sun-chairs at the hotel they'd rented, the pool itself was *indoors*. Which suited Dakota just fine. She could feel the persuasion of the air conditioned room. The private, hotel pool room smelled vaguely of chlorine. She spotted a couple of wet pool noodles floating on the water, along with an innertube. A couple of green, oversized lily pads ornamented the shallow end of the pool.

But currently, as evening was approaching, most of the hotel residents were at dinner, and the pool was temporarily empty.

Dakota exhaled as she glanced once again at her laptop screen, studying the information she'd entered into the database. She clicked her tongue and cycled to a new page of search results. "Got anything?" she said.

Marcus was also on his laptop, though he had laid a towel across his long legs to prevent any moisture from creeping into his battery. She'd been pretty sure this wasn't a thing that could happen, but Marcus had sounded adamant.

Now, the two of them settled in their sunchairs, brows furrowed.

"Not too many zoos in the immediate area," Dakota said quietly. "Killer targeted two women in a twenty mile radius. I went to fifty, and there are only six spots—a couple of park ranger stations an animal control operation and three zoos."

"Are you looking by company name for the tranquilizer?" Marcus said, glancing over.

"Yeah—see the coroner report? Bottom left. There's a list of companies that sell the compound in the chemicals he's using."

Marcus frowned, his fingers flying over the keys briefly. Then he muttered darkly beneath his breath. He never swore, but he said, "Crap," which was his version of an expletive. "Didn't see that. I thought we were looking for zoos in general."

Dakota just shook her head, returning her attention to the screen. "It's all this heat," she muttered. "It's getting to you."

"I... I'm still not seeing any specific results," Marcus said. "If you widen the parameters, it inundates the list. Plus, we don't actually know *which* chemical supplier he's getting his base components from. There's three on that list."

Dakota nodded, sighing. "Yeah... I guess I figured we'd take them one at a time."

Marcus hesitated. "Is there any way to find out *which* company sells which component?"

Dakota shook her head, looking over the top of her laptop. "Thought of that, but no. That information is kept tight. Could try calling, but you know how chemical labs are."

"Right... Hmm. Warrant?"

"Yeah... yeah I guess, we could go that route..." Dakota trailed off, but then clicked her fingers. "Actually, I might have an idea."

She fished her phone from her pocket, feeling a sudden bad taste in her mouth as she remembered the phone call with her father. But she pushed this thought aside and hastily entered a new number.

She shifted in the sun chair, feeling the thin plastic straps between the white poles press against her back. She tapped her fingers against the edge of her keyboard, the cold metal smooth against her skin as she waited for her phone to connect.

After the third ring, a voice.

"Hey, Dakota!" an energetic, excited voice.

She pictured smiling eyes, curling Cupid-hair and sweet dimples above a strong, masculine jaw. She shifted uncomfortably again, turning away from where Marcus was watching, amused. "Umm, hey, Mark," she said hesitantly. "I mean," she coughed, "Agent Bonet."

Mark chuckled. "Is Clement there?"

"Yes, yes, that sounds right," Dakota said, since her partner couldn't hear.

"What shirt is he wearing today?" Bonet asked, excited.

"Oh... Well, I guess I couldn't exactly say."

"Try me!" Bonet said.

She shot a look towards Marcus who was watching her with a quirked eyebrow. She turned back and said. "Umm, hmm... The suspect was a man wearing a red suit. He had dark glasses on."

"The suspect? I see. Don't think I know that one. Well, say high from me."

Dakota did not. She didn't want Marcus to think she was *too* familiar or friendly with Bonet. Though... she was. But she still wasn't sure what was going to come of it. So instead, clearing her throat, she said, hastily, "I—I actually was wondering if you could do me a favor."

"Oh," he said. "Nice. Work call?"

"Yeah. Yeah, I was wondering if you could look something up for me."

"Sure. Shoot."

She felt a flicker of relief that they'd managed to make it past the polite preamble without causing Marcus to pay *too* close of attention.

"So, we got some information from the coroner," Dakota said quickly, "that the tranquilizer the killer is using is the sort often used by big-game hunters, park rangers, and zoo employees. We're trying to locate *where* this particular compound was taken from. But the companies don't list exactly what type of chemicals they sell. If you could narrow down the list—that'd be very helpful."

"Sure," he said. "Can you send me the info?"

"Umm, right now?"

"Yeah—won't take a long time."

"Really?"

"Sure," he said, clearly trying to sound casual.

Part of Dakota wondered if he was trying to impress her. And another part of her wondered if she ought to tell him it was working.

She texted the information the coroner had sent them. "Those three chemical names. See them?"

"Yup. Got it. So you want to know what companies sell which ones?"

"Yes... If there are certain companies that don't supply *any* of the chemicals on that list, we can remove them from our search parameters."

"Perfect. Huh... well, right off," he said, "This middle one. Obsolete."

"How so?"

"Hasn't been sold in nearly twenty years. Outdated."

"Oh," Dakota said, pleasantly surprised. "That's good. So what about the other two?"

She didn't receive a reply at first, but she did hear the sound of fingers speeding over the keys on a keyboard. Marcus was still watching her. His eyebrow was still raised.

She shifted uncomfortably again. Even at the side of a swimming pool, she wore her long-sleeved turtleneck.

"Ah, okay," Bonet said after a moment. "So... there's a private sales list where they track inventory. Three of these companies stock the first chemical compound... Ah, but one of them does not sell locally. It's an export business."

"Alright... So are there any locations that *do* sell locally?"

More clacking keys. A long pause. Some murmuring. She half imagined what Bonet might look like. The athletic physique, his handsome silhouette, hunched over a keyboard, fingers flying. She smirked at the image, but then coughed delicately, trying to shift her thought patterns.

"Ah," he said suddenly. "Got it! Yeah, I've got three companies that sell one of those two drugs. All of them local. In about a hundred mile radius."

"Okay, and if we make it fifty?"

"Then... two companies."

Dakota was nodding now, feeling her excitement mounting. "And at those two companies... are there any employees with criminal records?"

"Umm... yes... but only one involved in distribution."

"One of the company's employees that would have access to the tranquilizer?"

"Well, one with a criminal record yeah... The guy is violent, but... huh, interesting."

"What's that?" she said, perking up.

"Looks like this guy's route actually took him through the supermarket where your second victim was killed. He... he wasn't dropping off tranquilizer. Looks like the company does beauty products too. But he stopped by the supermarket every couple of weeks."

Dakota felt a slow prickle of excitement. "Impressive," she said, trying to keep her voice in check. "Way to go!"

"Thanks—so... we on for this weekend?"

"Yes—yeah. I'm... looking forward to it."

She bid farewell then hung up, lowering her phone, and glancing towards where Agent Clement was casually examining his fingernails. "Looking forward to what?" he said in a playful tone.

"Finding our killer," she retorted, glaring.

"The suspect has a red suit and wearing sunglasses," Marcus replied. He glanced down at his shirt, then up at her. He pointed a large finger at her. "You're not half as subtle as you think."

Dakota's laptop lid closed with a *click*. She was already pushing to her feet. "Oh, don't worry. Mark, er, Agent Bonet likes your shirts. It's a compliment."

"I'm sure it is," Marcus said without a note of sarcasm.

He was also rising. "I take it by your reaction we have a lead."

"Yes," Dakota said. "One of the company distributors has a violent criminal record. And also," she said emphatically, "his route took him to Ms. Childs's workplace. She was killed in a supply closet on our suspect's route."

"What's the suspect's name?" Marcus said.

Dakota went still. She glanced down, frowned, then up again.

Marcus watched her now, eyes glinting. "You... you *did* get a name from *Mark* didn't you? You weren't *too* distracted by looking forward to anything to remember to get the name of the suspect who—"

"Shut up." Dakota pulled her phone out again, sheepishly.

It was testament to Agent Clement's trust in her that he was grinning. But as she marched out of the swimming pool area, laptop bag back in hand, she felt her frown creasing her brow.

"Get it together, Steele," she muttered beneath her breath. She'd forgotten to get the name of the damn suspect. She sighed. Maybe she wasn't being honest about exactly *how much* she liked Agent Bonet.

No... no that couldn't be it.

It was the heat.

The damn, Arizona heat.

CHAPTER EIGHT

"What was his name again?"

Dakota glared through the windshield, her teeth pressed together. "You know," she said, her voice gruff. "You're not as funny as you think you are."

Marcus just giggled from the front seat as he pulled down the street, following the GPS on the dashboard.

Dakota shot a final look towards the image of the man Agent Bonet had found.

Shawn Dardon. He had been working for Lone Leaf Pharmaceuticals for nearly ten months. In the past, he had served time for assaulting a woman at a bar. According to Mark, he had lied on his application to the company.

Dakota glanced through the windshield as they pulled into a driveway, staring up at the single-story house. She frowned, pointing to one of the windows. "That doesn't look good."

Marcus followed her indicating finger. He nodded once. "Do you think maybe Mr. Dardon is a violent man?"

It was a quip more than an observation. But she couldn't help but think Marcus was right. Something had been thrown through the window. And now, over the smashed glass, cardboard and duct tape had been used to plaster the broken portion.

The mood turned somber.

Dakota and Marcus exited their vehicle, slowly, eyes on the small home.

"No sign of his delivery truck," murmured Marcus.

"I doubt he takes it home with him."

The two of them now had their hands on their holsters.

Dakota had worn her shoulder strap, and so she unbuttoned her jacket to reach her gun. She didn't draw her weapon yet, but she mimed the motion, re-acclimating to the possibility.

Marcus looked uncomfortable as his fingers hovered over his own weapon.

Agent Clement had been forced to shoot a man on a previous case. He had saved a life in the process, but she knew her partner; he preferred saving lives to taking them. He had a big heart, even where criminals were concerned.

Dakota wished she had the same compassion as the big man

She didn't know where he had developed this perspective. Marcus had grown up in an upper middle-class home, raised by two doting parents. Occasionally, he would say things that made her wonder if there was more to that story but she had never pried. She didn't want to evoke return fire about her own past.

Now, she followed Marcus towards the front door of the small house.

"Shawn Dardon!" Marcus called out, his large hand pounding against the wooden door.

Dakota went still, listening. Marcus waited.

No response.

"Think he might not be home?" Marcus murmured.

Dakota glanced at the smashed window, her eyes moving to the driveway. There was a small garage, the red brick wall overgrown with long weeds. A green garden hose, that looked to have been run over more than once, draped across the driveway. A faint stream of water leaked from the garden hose, slowly staining the driveway, and spilling down towards the gutter.

Dakota knocked on the door now. "FBI!" she called out, her voice loud. "Mr. Dardon, open up!"

"Go away!" a voice shouted. A trembling, timid voice.

A second later, Dakota heard something else.

The sound sent shivers down her spine. She tensed, and stared at the door. "Did you hear that?" She muttered beneath her breath.

"The growl?" Marcus muttered. He shifted uncomfortably on the concrete step. He cleared his throat. "Mr. Dardon, is everything okay?"

Another yelp. "Please, go away." The voice sounded panicked. But also strained, as if exerting itself in some physical way.

Dakota couldn't even imagine what was happening on the other side of that door. Part of her didn't want to find out. She could hear the thing growling from within the house. A dog?

"Damn it," she muttered. She reached out, trying the door handle. Locked.

"You're riling it up," the man shouted. "Go away, please. You're riling it up!"

"Don't like the sound of that," Marcus muttered.

Dakota was shaking her head, wondering if it was bad form to allow her partner to enter the house first.

But in the end, the two of them both backed up, shared a look, and simultaneously stepped forward and kicked out, hard.

Marcus was far larger than she was. But Dakota had learned how to kick properly. One of her best weapons, when fighting, had been her kicks. Especially to the body. And now, as their feet connected with the door, they shattered the flimsy material, and sent it crashing open.

The two of them stood on the concrete step, staring into the house.

"Nope," Marcus yelped. He slammed the door shut a second after it flung open.

Dakota did not blame him. She stared at her partner, standing on the other side of the rapidly closed door. The growling had come closer now. She thought she heard the sound of claws against tile.

"Was that a tiger?" she said, staring at Marcus.

"Yes. Yes, I believe that was a tiger. Mr. Dardon," Marcus said, louder again. "Sir, are you aware you have a tiger in your house?"

"It's just a cat," the voice came back. It sounded desperate now.

Dakota cleared her throat. She shifted uncomfortably on the concrete step. "Sir, just to observe, by the tone of your voice, it suggests to me that you know you're not allowed to have a tiger in your house."

"Please, you're too loud. You're making him angry."

Marcus hesitated. "An angry tiger. Of all the things. An *angry* tiger."

Dakota shrugged. "We're not technically here for the tiger. We could leave that to –"

"Animal control. Perfect. They love pawning jurisdiction off on–"

"Us. Right. That's what I'm saying."

They both glanced at each other, shared another look, and turned back to the door. Simultaneously, they both called out, "Mr. Dardon?"

"I really mean it," the same timid voice said. "Agh—down *Stripes!* Get down."

"Sir, we need you to come out here with us, please. Just approach the door, and come out with your hands up."

"Go away! He doesn't like the loud noises."

Dakota scratched her chin. "You mean like this?" she shouted.

She heard cursing from inside. "Stripes, sit. No. No, stop chewing that."

Dakota tried knocking on the door, loudly. "What about this?" she shouted.

More cursing. The sound of rapid footsteps.

Marcus shrugged at Dakota, and joined in. He pounded his fist against the door. "Mr. Dardon, FBI. Open up."

"Dammit. Idiots. Stop." The door suddenly opened, and a panicked, gasping small man slipped out into the fading sunlight of the Arizona heat.

He glanced between the two agents, scowling deeply. "Think you're funny?"

Dakota pointed past him, and Marcus was busy shutting the door. "No," she said, "I think that's funny. Because I thought I saw a *tiger*."

He shifted uncomfortably. "It's perfectly safe. I trained him since he was a cub. Look, please, he's the only friend I have."

Marcus looked instantly sympathetic. Dakota, though, glared. "Sir, I'm afraid you're going to have to come with us." The sympathy did not work for Dakota. She had seen what Mr. Dardon had done to that woman he'd assaulted all those years ago. She had seen what someone had been doing to the most recent victims. And at the top of their list of suspects, they were facing a man with a comb-over, wearing a polka dot bowtie, and a fleece sweater covered with long strands of tiger hair.

She double checked that the door was shut. Then, winced at Marcus. "Maybe you should put that in front, just in case."

Marcus nodded quickly, bent over the railing of the steps, and grabbed a trashcan near a recycling bin next to the concrete steps. He pulled the thing, and placed it in front of the door.

"Now," Mr. Dardon was saying hurriedly, "It's fine. He's perfectly safe. He's just getting antsy with all the yelling."

"It looked like he was eating a pillow," Dakota pointed out.

"Well, yes, I suppose he was. Now, please, what's this about?"

But now with the door barricaded, Marcus began to push Mr. Dardon down the steps. He was polite about it, but firm.

Dakota pulled her phone from her pocket, still shooting looks back towards the door, as growling sounds escaped.

She shook her head, muttering in absolute amazement.

When the phone was answered on the other end, she cleared her throat. "This is Agent Dakota Steele, BAU. I've got an interesting one for you. How far are you from this address..." She rattled off the house and street number, and then she took the steps as well, following after Marcus, and hastening towards the rental car.

CHAPTER NINE

At least this precinct, thanks to the cooling effect of the evening, wasn't sweltering. But now, as Dakota settled across from Mr. Dardon, her eyes on the thin man, she could feel the attention of the camera in the corner of the room.

She glanced up at the blinking red light, frowned, then looked down again.

The police officers in the Arizona precinct had heard about the tiger. She supposed they were going to be tonight's entertainment.

Agent Marcus Clement was pulling up a metal chair, and once seated, he folded his hands and stared across the table. "Mr. Dardon," Marcus said slowly, "do you know why you're here?"

Dardon was shifting uncomfortably, glancing side to side and nibbling at the corner of his lip.

He cleared his throat at this comment, and gave a quick, furtive shake of his head. "Absolutely not," he said hurriedly. "Is Stripes okay?"

Dakota leaned in now as she had been the one coordinating with animal control.

"Your tiger is being transported right now, sir. You do know it's illegal to own it as a pet, don't you?"

Mr. Dardon gave a weak little sigh, exhaling softly. "It's a magnificent creature. I got him for a really good deal."

"I'm afraid that doesn't make it any more legal."

He frowned across the table. "Where are they taking him?"

Marcus frowned quizzically at Mr. Dardon. "Sir, if I were you, I'd be a bit more concerned about myself."

He swallowed, examining the large agent, then shifted uncomfortably, shrugging one shoulder. His handcuffed wrists pressed against each other, as if he were testing the temerity of the metal. "What is this all about? You broke down my door," he added in an accusatory voice.

Dakota examined the man. She had a gift for paying attention to details. She wasn't someone who had enjoyed her time in school though she'd managed to get her GED after a few years exploring the world. By the time she made it to college, and through a course in criminal justice, she had known that her best skillset had come from her training as a fighter.

People did not lie in the cage. They might bluff. Their postures might communicate something dishonest. They would fake and juke. But they couldn't lie. Eventually, beneath the bright lights, with fists and fury, fighters would sort out who was the real deal, and who was faking.

And as she watched Mr. Dardon, she had the sense that this was a man who knew he was in trouble. And he was playing a role. Timid, eager, nervous...

So instead of letting him get away with it, she said, "Mr. Dardon, is it true that you assaulted a woman over a dispute in a bar?"

He shifted uncomfortably. "I served my sentence for that. I got eight months. That was years ago."

"And yet you lied on your application to your current company, didn't you?"

He scratched uncomfortably at his chin, his other hand rising, attached by the handcuff. "Man, it's hard out there. I just needed a job."

She frowned. He was still speaking in a sort of "aw shucks, oh jeez" tone. She said, "You fractured her eye socket, sir."

He shook his head hurriedly. "She fell. I pushed her, but she fell. Besides, she dumped a drink down my shirt."

Marcus said, "We're not here about a previous altercation. Yes, you served your time. But, I'm afraid we need to ask you about Billie Childs."

He leaned back. He wrinkled his nose. "Who?"

"She worked at one of the large Cut-Price supermarkets you deliver to."

"I deliver a lot of places. And I don't make a habit of speaking with the employees there. It's a job, not a soirée."

Dakota now glimpsed a little bit of the other side of Mr. Dardon. The snarky, sarcastic side. The side that disdained the cops that had come to his door. The side that assaulted a woman. That purchased an illegal tiger. That sat across the table, pretending to be one thing, as if certain the FBI was too stupid to realize.

She didn't blink, didn't accuse, just sat, straight-postured, attentive. Now that she knew he was pretending, it gave an advantage. In a fight in the ring, finding opponents' weaknesses wasn't always useful until you took them deep. The more tired and distracted they were, the easier it was to exploit.

So now, she said, simply.

"Did you have any interaction with Ms. Childs?"

"I just told you I don't know who that is."

"Is it true that you transport a tranquilizer as part of your delivery route?"

He shrugged. "I just deliver; I have an itinerary and an inventory. I let the people at the companies check the numbers on the crates. That's it."

"You wouldn't be lying to us, would you?"

"Lying about what?"

"Sir," Marcus said, slowly, "perhaps if we show you a picture of the woman."

The man shrugged.

Marcus pulled out his phone and slid it across the table. Dakota watched closely. The image on the screen was of their second victim.

"She was a graduate student," Marcus said slowly. "Do you recognize her?"

The man leaned in, studying the phone. He wrinkled his nose, and said, "I don't remember."

Dakota studied him. He thought he was smarter, more prepared. She could see right through the act. He was small, with a comb-over but he had cold eyes.

Still, that did not mean he was their killer.

"I watched the footage," she said simply.

"What?"

"I watched the footage of your interaction in that bar. The woman accidentally spilled a drink. And then you slammed her head against the counter. Is that about right?"

He frowned at her, eyes narrowing. He said, "The angle you watched must have made it difficult to see."

"It didn't seem difficult to me," Dakota said slowly. She pushed out of her chair now, walking away, and standing by the door. She was simply displaying her freedom of motion. Dardon was cuffed, unable to move. Something like this might trigger a man like that. She said, simply, "Do you need me to get you anything?"

He hesitated, then frowned at her.

She clicked her tongue. "Do the cuffs hurt?"

Marcus shot her a look, but didn't comment, allowing her to take the lead.

Mr. Dardon was leaning back now. Scowling.

Dakota said, "I could get you a booster chair if you like."

"What the hell is this?" He snapped. Some of his flustered,

stumbling way of speaking vanished now.

She smiled. Quickly, she covered. She said, "I don't mean to upset you, Mr. Dardon."

He was glaring at her—his lips pressed in a thin line.

"What would you do," she said softly, "if you and I were alone in here? And those cuffs were off you. Would you attack me like you did that woman? Would you try to slam my head into the table?"

Marcus had grown to trust Dakota over the years. He was frowning, though. Still, while he had the bedside manner, Dakota could spot sharks in the water. This man was playing a role.

After a few moments, glaring at her, he swallowed faintly, and leaned back. "I didn't kill anyone," he said softly.

She pointed at him. "Do you know Ms. Childs?"

He scratched his chin again. "Do you have someone that says I do?"

The mention of the security footage had spooked him. She had intended to communicate omniscience. She knew things that he didn't realize. By doing this, it could often incite a suspect to confess things that weren't known. It was an old trick. Used by mothers everywhere, to convince their children that they might as well come clean, because she knew anyway.

Now, the man was fidgeting. He was scowling still. "Fine," he said. "Was it Demi? Did she say I knew her? Look, it wasn't anything. I only asked her out the one time."

Dakota went stiff. Marcus raised his eyebrows, impressed.

Dakota just said, "And what happened then?"

"Nothing. That was it. I thought she was cute, and she said no. I didn't do anything. Is that what this is about? I saw the news. You think I killed her."

"Did you?"

"Hell no. I'm too busy taking care of Stripes. He needs me. Besides, I don't have the time. I worked two shifts."

Dakota shot a look at Marcus. The tall man, though, said, "Were you working Tuesday?"

Dardon was scowling between the two of them, his voice thick with frustration. "Hell yeah. I worked every day this week. I don't get breaks. Not unless I'm dragged off to a police station."

Now the resentment, the bitterness was coming out.

Dakota hesitated, though, glancing to Marcus. The same way he often gave her latitude, because he knew her style, she also knew him. And now he looked troubled.

He said, "So you've been working eighty hours for the last week?"

40

"Try the last few months," he retorted. "It's not easy keeping an exotic animal."

Marcus sighed. "Alright, Mr. Dardon, I'm going to verify that with your company."

Dakota stared as Marcus pushed up, and turned to her.

She frowned. The man was clearly lying. But Marcus walked past her, gesturing for her to join him in the hall.

She stepped out of the interrogation room, grateful to leave those glaring eyes, and the watchful camera. As she stepped into the corridor, though, and the door clicked shut behind her, Marcus looked at her. "Those cameras record twenty-four seven," he said.

"Wait, what cameras?"

He said, "The ones on the trucks. Weren't you listening in the car?"

"I was on hold with animal control. What cameras, Marcus?"

He sighed, probing the bridge of his nose. "The cameras in the delivery vehicle that our suspect drives. There is a dash camera but also a cabin camera. It would show him on the road. If he's been traveling for eighty hours, this week, there's no way that he was the one involved in the murders."

"I mean, it's possible that he took a break somewhere."

"Our victim was killed in the morning, during work hours. Which means we would see on the truck when he shows up."

Dakota frowned. "Maybe he got out of the vehicle."

"It's possible. But like I said, there's cameras on the dash too. There's also camera in the rear. So if he was there, loading boxes, there's no way he was in the building attacking our victim."

Dakota stared. She felt her stomach twist. She shifted uncomfortably on the cold tiled floor. "Worth checking the footage," she said.

Marcus nodded.

"Your turn," she said.

Now he frowned.

"I did animal control," she protested. "It's your turn."

Marcus rolled his eyes, and Dakota could feel her own frown forming. Neither of them was upset with the other. But the inference was clear. If he really was in a truck for eighty hours, being tracked by cameras, there would inevitably be an alibi for at least one of the murders.

But maybe he was lying.

Dakota hissed in frustration. He would have to be lying. Because if not, then they had the wrong guy in the interrogation room; the killer was still out there.

Suddenly, Dakota tensed—her phone was ringing. She reached down, lifting the device, her forehead furrowed. "Yes?" she answered.

She paused, listening. She swallowed. Marcus stared at her, his eyes piercing. "What's the matter?" he murmured.

She lowered the phone slowly, nodding a single time. "Another body. Shit."

CHAPTER TEN

Marcus tapped against the steering wheel, fidgeting uncomfortably as he pulled into the parking lot of the gas station. Flashing red and blue lights strobed across greasy windows. The different fuel pumps were blockaded by police vehicles.

Marcus stared in the direction of the gas station, frowning. The vehicle came to a stop, crossing over the white lines. He glanced towards Dakota who was already unbuckling and reaching for the lock. She'd been quiet ever since they'd received the footage confirming Mr. Dardon's alibi. Not once had he left his vehicle while unloading at the second victim's supermarket.

The suspect was in the clear... Not to mention...

Another body while Dardon had been in custody.

Marcus could feel a slow prickle of anxiety. Often, he'd spend time in the gym, lifting heavy things in order to keep his mind focused. But when traveling for a case, it broke his routine. He glanced at the small dash-can that Dakota had purchased for him years ago.

At first, it had been a bit of a joke to bring it with him and place it in their loaned vehicles.

Now, though, it had become something of a fixture in his life.

Dakota had bought the small, dashboard trashcan so he could throw gum wrappers inside, after leaving a couple on the floor during one case. She had a predilection for cleanliness. For appearance.

He appreciated this about her.

He put the vehicle in park, noticing the way Dakota was already opening the door and pushing out into the gas station parking lot.

Dakota wasn't the sort to slow down on a case like this. He was glad to have her back. Her drive, her unrelenting focus, helped him.

He stepped out of the vehicle now, too, noticing where a man in a wide-brim hat was waving them over. The man stood behind a small barricade of glass and reinforced plastic—it resembled something of an oversized blast shield.

The man in the hat was peering at a computer monitor, pointing at something and listening as another man in a blue fleece was murmuring comments about the screen.

Dakota was already making a beeline towards the gathering behind the screen. Marcus fell into step as well. He caught up with Dakota in time to hear the man in the round hat introduce himself. "Milo Marsters, Homeland Security. You must be Agent Steele." He didn't offer his hand. In fact, Marcus noticed the man was wearing protective gloves.

Dakota nodded, then pointed to Marcus. "And this is Agent Clement."

Marcus received a quick head bob as well. The man from Homeland Security was wearing a clean-pressed suit and had silver sideburns. His upper lip displayed a small film of prickling white—not quite a mustache, but an attempt. His eyes kept darting about, moving back to the monitor, to the agents, then the monitor again.

Marcus, who was accustomed to taking the lead in their partnership when speaking with strangers, cleared his throat. "So we were told she was found in the bathroom."

"Yup, yup," said Marsters, nodding quickly. He waved a hand towards the bathroom. Clement watched where two figures in hazmat suits were feeding a camera through a vent above the door to a gas station bathroom.

Marsters directed their attention to the computer monitor behind the screen. He moved with erratic, jerking motions. His finger tapped the screen, leaving a smudge where it trailed. He muttered to himself, tried to wipe the smudge, but only made things worse.

The man sighed in frustration but then continued as if nothing had happened as the two FBI agents joined him. "We're treating the situation as hazardous. Your victim is there," he said. "My priority, though, right now, is to make sure no one *else* gets harmed."

"Is that her, there?" Dakota said curtly, pointing as well. She made as if to begin moving around the screen, towards the bathroom.

But Marsters clicked his tongue. "Wait, wait," he said quickly. He caught Dakota by the wrist, giving her a quick tug back.

Dakota turned sharply, looking at the hand holding her. The man must have noticed something in her gaze, because he coughed delicately and immediately released his grip on her wrist. "Apologies," he said hurriedly. "But I haven't cleared the scene yet."

Dakota glanced at Marcus. Agent Clement nodded slowly. He said, "So what is it we know then?"

But Marsters was pointing at the screen again, more insistently now. Dakota and Marcus both leaned in, watching as the team in hazmat suits were slowly, cautiously, entering the gas station bathroom now. Marcus could hear voices as officers behind them redirected foot traffic.

On the screen, in real-time, they watched as the figures pressed into the bathroom, moving slowly. A video feed displayed the victim sprawled across the tiled floor. The camera moved slowly, showing grainy footage. Marcus's gaze darted over the screen, towards the room beyond, but was having difficulty tracking the location of the surveying team, so he returned his full attention to the video feed. He felt a slow, rising sense of trepidation, but he held back the fear... He'd never worked a case quite like this before... but that was the job. Unusual cases. Still... he'd sleep better once this guy was behind bars.

They all watched in silence as the camera lingered on the body.

"Have you identified her yet?" Dakota asked.

Marsters nodded once. He waved a hand towards a car parked outside the station. "Ran the plates. A Donna Windser."

"Do we know anything about Ms. Windser?" Dakota said, her eyes narrowed as she stared at the screen.

The man just shook his head, though. "Not much yet. She was found dead inside three hours ago. Someone spotted a nozzle attached to a canister in the vent—ah, yes, see."

He was tapping a portion of the left wall, visible on the video feed. Marcus frowned, unable to make out much in the dingy footage.

But Dakota seemed to notice it, judging by the sharp hiss of her breath. "He gassed her, then?" she said. "Do we know if the chemicals are still lingering?"

"They're checking now," Marsters replied quietly. "The killer rigged the door and used his little trap..."

"He was waiting for her," Dakota replied.

"Hmm?"

"He must have scoped out the area first—had time to set up. He was waiting for her."

Marsters shook his head. "The cannister was lodged there—could have taken only a few moments."

"So you think the victim was random?"

Marsters shrugged. "Not my area, agents. Now, if you don't mind, it's going to take some time to clear the scene. So if you could..." He trailed off, wincing apologetically and waving a hand for them to retreat.

Dakota frowned at this hand—the same hand that had snatched her wrist, but Marcus scooped an arm around her back and gently began to guide her away. He knew his partner could often have a single-track mind when it came to these cases. She so badly wanted to catch the

45

killer that she didn't often appreciate bureaucratic oversight or obstacles.

He'd once seen her drive off a small overpass into a wheat field and across it, in order to avoid a traffic jam.

Marcus, on the other hand, tried to play nice with others.

"Why don't we speak with the gas station manager," Marcus murmured as he led her away. "He might have seen something. Plus cameras."

Dakota puffed air, but then nodded quickly. As they moved away from the bathroom, they made a beeline towards a police vehicle sitting on the other side of the gas station, behind a sawhorse barrier. The man was wearing a uniform that matched the colors of the gas station, and had a nametag. He was an older gentleman and judging by his frustrated motions, Marcus pegged him as either the owner or manager.

Most low-level gas station attendants weren't so insistent on getting back to work.

Dakota's expression had morphed now. Instead of frustrated, she looked calm. He'd always admired her ability to keep her emotions in check. At the same time, this skill of his partner's sometimes scared him.

The two of them moved swiftly across the asphalt towards the man sitting in the back of the police SUV. His legs were dangling out the open door, and a finger was flailing in circles as he berated the officer who'd been unlucky enough to earn the babysitting gig.

As the gas-station manager's voice began to rise, though, he suddenly surged to his feet, and tried to march past the sawhorse.

The second he did this, though, the cop in question shoved him *hard,* sending him stumbling over the wooden sawhorse.

Clearly, the cop assigned to babysitting duty had already received more than his share of berating. But as he lashed out, the gas-station manager yelled, stumbling over the wooden barrier.

As the man toppled, with a shout, Dakota bolted forward. Marcus jogged a few steps to keep up.

Dakota caught the man as he surged to his feet, furious. The cop was already reaching for handcuffs. Marcus hastened between the two. "Hang on—cut it out!" Marcus said quickly.

Dakota was frowning at the cop. "You shoved him," she said.

"He tried to cross the boundary," the cop retorted.

"So you pushed him over it?" Dakota returned, scowling.

Marcus sighed. This was always the worst part of a high-pressure job. He helped Dakota lift the gas-station manager back to his feet.

Marcus's eyes darted down to spot the name of the man written in small, black letters on his silver nametag. *Garesh.*

"Garesh?" Dakota said also noting the name. She brushed him off. "Apologies."

The man was spluttering, shaking his head side to side. He had a thick, black beard and eyes that kept narrowing whenever he glanced at one of the LEOs. He was still shaking his finger, this time pointing it towards Dakota. "Hoodlums!" he exclaimed. "Thieves! I've been closed for half the day! I've lost all my business. And this... this *thug* attacks me!"

"Hey, bud," snapped the officer, "Watch it!"

Dakota turned on the cop. "You watch it!" she snapped.

"Dakota," Marcus said with a sigh. "How about we all just calm down."

The cop, the manager, and his partner all turned to him and glared. He shifted uncomfortably. "I guess not then," he muttered beneath his breath.

Marcus went quiet, trying his best not to interject further as his input clearly wasn't wanted.

"How about you get back in your car," Dakota said, addressing the cop firmly, "and let us interview the witness."

The officer glared at her. The manager, still seething, tried to protest, but Dakota, turned sharply, and by sheer force of will redirected the manager's attention to her. Marcus, following the lead, stepped in, wincing apologetically at the police officer, and gesturing towards his vehicle. At the same time, Marcus flashed his identification and his badge.

The police officer turned away, muttering darkly, shaking his head, and marching off.

Dakota, unaware of this now, was addressing the manager. "I apologize for the inconvenience," she said quickly.

"You're costing me hundreds of dollars," he retorted. "It's not inconvenience. It's theft."

Dakota nodded once. She was no longer frowning. Again, Marcus marveled at the way his partner could sometimes let her emotions loose, and seconds later bottle them up, hiding them completely from view. But he knew her; he knew Dakota *well*. They had been partners for a decade before that calamity four months ago. The case with The Watcher. A woman had died. A woman who didn't need to die. The killer had gotten away. He hadn't been active since then, but Marcus wasn't optimistic that they had seen the last of the murderer.

47

And yet, with Dakota, he couldn't help but feel a strong fondness for her. He knew she struggled with alcohol. Knew she struggled with other things besides.

But Marcus saw a bit of himself in Dakota. For the first ten years of his life, Agent Clement had been raised by his parents. In a broken, downtrodden part of a forgotten city block. He could have named most illegal drugs by the age of eight. Tragedy had struck his family but for Marcus, it had almost been a gift.

He'd been taken in by his aunt and uncle. Overnight, his prospects had changed. His life had changed. They had been gracious, gentle, God-fearing people. They had taken care of Marcus as if he were their own. Marcus had been sent to private school, been educated. He had played sports, and stayed out of trouble.

He had grown up protected and sheltered.

But he had always known, if not for his aunt and uncle, he easily could have been just another statistic. Young boys from the city, with parents in and out of jail, didn't often have the chance to make it as far as he had.

Dakota, he knew, had grown up rough. Her own family had fallen apart, especially after the disappearance of her sister. Marcus did not pry about that part of Dakota's life. He didn't think it was his responsibility.

If ever she wanted to talk, he would have been more than willing to listen. But Agent Clement knew that if not for his aunt and uncle, he would have had a much tougher life. He saw Dakota as something of a hero. She had made it out of a dangerous portion of Rapid City, using her combat sport as handholds up a mountain.

An alcohol issue and a few questionable tattoos were a small price to pay to escape.

And so Marcus did not mind following his partner's lead. Marcus hadn't wanted Dakota back, after she had quit three months ago, just because she was good at her job. But also because he cared for her.

Dakota was hope. He had often feared that if not for his aunt and uncle, his life would have inevitably ended far worse. But Dakota gave him hope. That even out of rough circumstances, without some guardian angels swooping in, someone could make something of their life.

Now, he watched as Agent Steele, using her usual curt tone, said, "Can we look at those cameras?"

"Which cameras?"

"The ones above the door. That one."

"No, I see where you're pointing. But that camera isn't recording. It's a fake. It's not even hooked up to anything."

Dakota frowned. "A fake camera?"

The manager nodded. "A deterrence. That's it. There is no footage."

"Are you lying?"

He looked taken aback by the direct accusation. But Dakota was often direct. He frowned. "No. Go look at it for yourself. There isn't even a wire out the back. It's not on. I don't have batteries in it."

"Fine, I believe you," she said quickly.

He muttered to himself, shaking his head furiously.

She said, "Anything else you could add? Did you see anything a few hours ago?"

"I see a lot of things. You're going to have to be more specific."

Before she could continue further, though, there was a sudden sound of thumping. Then rapid footsteps and muttered voices. Marcus turned, frowning and watching as the figures emerged from the gas station bathroom, removing their hazmat suits. A woman with blonde hair streaked in gray was shaking her head, addressing Marsters. "It's safe," she called out. "Coroner and lab can access now."

Marsters flashed a thumbs up.

Marcus let out a faint breath of air. He watched as a corpse beneath a white blanket was slowly being wheeled out on a stretcher.

CHAPTER ELEVEN

Dakota watched the figures emerge, pushing the stretcher with their latest victim. She could feel her stomach twist, could feel her emotions threatening to rebel against the horrible visual image. She hated this part of the job. Hated this part of *life*.

The seeming inevitability of death. And of her helplessness in the face of it.

She turned sharply, swallowing briefly and facing Garesh.

"Sir," she said, trying to keep her voice as steady as possible. She could feel where Agent Clement was watching her from the side. "Did you notice anyone lingering in your parking lot? Did anyone come in earlier that caught your attention?"

The manager gave a quick shake of his head. "Nothing," he said.

Dakota shifted in frustration, moving from one foot to the other. Normally, she let Agent Clement do most of the talking. She preferred the more physical parts of the job, chasing down suspects, beating up bad guys. But she also prided herself on being able to pay attention to details.

And so now, focusing, she watched the manager.

Bodies didn't lie the same as tongues. He was fidgeting, his fingers twitching. His cheeks were red. His eyes kept narrowing whenever he glanced at someone in a police uniform. This was a man who was not particularly fond of policemen. But also, he was more angry than nervous.

Not the posture of someone hiding something. Rather, the posture of someone who wished to lodge grievances.

Dakota decided to change direction. She said, "Did anything else happen? Did the woman who owned that car," she pointed to the sedan that Homeland Security had indicated, "Buy anything?"

The manager snorted. "People rarely stop in the shop nowadays. No, she didn't. Is that all? When are you leaving?"

Dakota shook her head. She kept her tone as calm as possible. "I don't know exactly. But, she said hurriedly, "We will get you back into your store as soon as possible, sir."

She noticed, off by the bathroom, that the body was now being attended to by two figures, where they adjusted straps, the blanket, and

50

began to wheel it towards an ambulance.

Other figures were loathe, it seemed, to enter the bathroom. They were wearing strange gas masks, and frowning at each other. None of them seemed interested in braving the toxic nature of a gas station bathroom.

"It's like something out of a bad movie," said the manager, shaking his head and muttering. He turned away, pulling his phone from his pocket, as the device made a quiet buzzing sound. He held up an irritated finger to Dakota, as if silencing her, then raised the phone, speaking hurriedly in a language Dakota did not understand.

She frowned, watching after him, but letting him go. Clearly, he didn't want to talk, nor did it seem like he had seen anything.

She sighed, glancing at Marcus, then shaking her head. "Think the coroner's going to find anything new?" she asked.

"We'll see," Marcus replied, watching her closely and giving a weary shrug. "Hard to think what at this point. What sort of man uses the vents of a gas station bathroom to poison a victim?"

Dakota shook her head. She pointed at his own phone which he now had in his hand. "Looking her up?"

Marcus nodded once. "Donna Windser," he murmured, frowning at his phone. "She just graduated high school."

Dakota winced. "Shit. Dammit. I hate that."

Marcus sighed. "There's no connection between the victims... What does the killer want?"

Dakota considered this comment, but didn't have anything to say. She just gave a weary shrug, and a quick shake of her head. "It sounded like this attack could have been random. Unless he followed her to a gas station."

"Why would he do that?"

"Maybe he wanted it in public. If you think about it, all of these murders have been risky. The last one, he was even seen by the manager."

"He was *barely* seen," Marcus said.

"He's avoiding cameras, but almost seems to want the attention." Dakota waved a hand at the crime scene. "I mean, just look around."

As Marcus glanced about, his eyes moving from one figure to the next, Dakota began walking past the sawhorse, back towards their parked vehicle. A coroner's report would take some time. She wasn't interested in walking into a gas station bathroom filled with potentially hazardous chemicals. Besides, she had seen what she needed to on the video footage.

Something else was sticking out to her.

Something that the manager said. This was like a scene out of a bad movie.

The manager had reacted as if in some déjà vu. Which had gotten her thinking, what if this crime wasn't as unique as she thought? What if it had happened before?

This thought propelled her forward. She reached the front of their borrowed vehicle. Through the slightly lowered window, she spotted the dash trashcan she had once purchased for Marcus, which he now brought with them on the plane in his luggage.

She had always appreciated Agent Clement. She was glad to be working with him again. She shot a look towards the tall, musclebound bodybuilder. He was following after. He wasn't the type that needed to take the lead. She had also appreciated this about him.

He was the backbone of their operation. A steady, calm voice of reason. She had often envied how he had grown up. Protected, safe. She didn't know much about his earlier days. But she knew he had been raised with money, and sent to only the best schools.

Most people like that made her feel like dirt. Marcus was the only one who she had ever gotten along with. And he went out of his way to make it clear that he did not think he was better than her.

Now, as she peered through the vehicle, she pulled her phone and began to type.

Chemical attack. Serial killer uses gas. Chemical killer. Multiple victims gas attack.

She tried different search parameters. Occasionally entering the information into various online news sources. But, more often than not, entering it into a broader search bar.

She leaned against the hood of the vehicle. The scent of gasoline lingered on the air. The general murmuring and hubbub mingled. Occasionally, traffic would swish by outside the gas station. Drivers would blare their horns, propelling rubbernecks forward who were lingering to watch the strange scene and the flashing lights.

Dakota tried to drown all of this out, focusing.

She tried more search terms. She moved along the results, studying both news articles and blog posts.

But nothing was coming up.

Again, she tried a new combination of the same words. And again, nothing in the news. She went back a decade. A few murders, and serial killers had some similarities. But none of them fit this MO.

She was feeling frustration. She went to the next page of search results, and again glimpsed a fictional story on a blog. She muttered darkly, shaking her head. She moved on to the next search result.

Nothing. Gibberish. Unrelated news articles. And there, another blog post.

She tried to move past, but then paused. Marcus was now leaning against the vehicle as well. It swayed, shifting from his weight.

But Dakota was fixating on the search result in the center of the page.

Another fictional article. An online serial novel.

The same article from earlier search results.

The website was called, *True Novelty—a look into the mind of darkness.*

Most of the title was cut off. She was forced to hover over it, to read the full, wordy mouthful.

She clicked the link. It was clearly labeled as fiction. A story. Not that it would help much. But the manager's comments came back. Like something out of a movie. What about a book? More specifically, what about an online serial novel?

She could feel her skin prickling. Could feel her sense of anticipation mounting.

She scanned the page.

"What is it?" Marcus murmured.

She gave a faint shake, trying to focus.

"Dakota, what's wrong?" Marcus said, leaning in now.

She said, "Listen to this: *the struggle... then silence. She lay draped inside the supply closet, one hand extending towards the door, her lips curled in a soundless scream... The poison had reached her lungs.*"

Dakota looked up.

Marcus wrinkled his nose. "A bit dramatic for an article. But I've heard worse."

"It's not from a news article."

He stared at her. "That sounds like our last victim. Where is it from?"

But Dakota was now tapping her phone excitedly. "Listen to this," she said, hurriedly, "*And there she lay, on the cold tile floor. The breath stolen from her lungs... choked... The scent of diesel fumes on the air, drifting through the vent behind the gas station.*"

Marcus was frowning now. "I... I don't understand. That's *not* a news article?" He glanced over his shoulder back in the direction of the gas station bathroom.

But Dakota could feel her skin prickling. "It was posted three days ago, Marcus. And the first one was posted a week before."

"Someone is predicting the murders?"

"Predicting, or scripting," she said firmly.

Marcus frowned. "Do you think our killer is bold enough to confess like this?"

"He has been killing in public places," she said with a shrug. "He clearly thinks he is smarter than us."

Marcus was shaking his head now. He looked frustrated. "Does our online mystery author have a name?"

Dakota had already been scrolling to the "about" section on the website banner. It took her to a single page of text. No image. But there was a name. "Cleveland Bryant."

Marcus was already on his own phone. She watched as his large fingers flew across the surface, entering the information in their database.

Once he was finished, he looked up. "Wow," he said slowly, "I think I have him. He only lives twenty minutes from here. Cleveland Bryant, not a very common name. I have him listed here is a coroner's assistant."

"A coroner's assistant?"

"No, hang on. IRS had him there for the last seven years. But last year, he stopped."

Marcus raised an eyebrow at her. And it was like passing the baton. Now, it was Dakota's turn to hastily text. Again, she was searching news articles. But this time, using the name of the online blogger, and adding "coroner's assistant."

And this time, using her coordinates to help localize the news, the article popped up almost instantly.

Dakota read the title to her partner, "Coroner's assistant fired—thief!" She read the article quickly, her eyes skimming from paragraph to paragraph. At last, she looked up. "Shit," she said slowly. "Our wannabe author was fired from his last job... The article is a political hit piece about the local DA... But it looks like Mr. Bryant was suspected of stealing from his workplace."

"From the coroner's?"

"Some sort of lab. Nothing was ever proven... so he wasn't arrested... but..." Dakota shrugged, looking up. "Think maybe we should visit Mr. Bryant?"

Marcus glanced across the gas station towards the ambulance. "Want to wait to hear what they find?"

Dakota shook her head. "They can let us know on the way. I don't want to just sit here, standing behind red tape."

Marcus nodded, already fishing his keys from his pocket as he rounded the hood of their car, picking up the pace to match the urgency in her tone.

CHAPTER TWELVE

Supervising Agent Carter frowned as her phone rang. She stared at the caller-ID, certain it was a mistake.

She hesitated behind her large walnut desk. Her feet were planted firmly on the floor. She didn't lean back, didn't believe in recliners. The more time it took to plant her feet, the less time she had to react to a threat.

The cameras in her room weren't so much to keep an eye out while she was present, but rather to keep watch when she went home for the evening. She always had the security team sweep her car before she left as well.

The faint, glowing light from the sun lamp by the window illuminated the large, black drapes which she'd custom ordered to fit her office window. The fabric was lined with strands of Kevlar. The window itself was bulletproof.

But one could never be *too* careful.

She massaged slowly at her left eye, wincing as she did. Most people didn't notice it was a fake eye. Didn't notice the cosmetic procedures used to smooth the skin along the left side of her face. If they looked closely—which she never allowed them to—they might notice the scarring behind her ear. The fact that her left ear was slightly smaller than her right... They hadn't managed to find all the pieces when stitching her face back together.

The bomb had been placed outside the government building where she'd worked before.

This *new* assignment, in no small part, was due to her actions on that day, twenty-five years ago. Many, many surgeries since then had been attempted to replace and repair and remove.

But the eye was gone. The skin numb. No sensation in her cheek.

But now, the sensation she felt was a jolt of anger.

The phone continued to ring.

Why was *he* calling her?

She let it go to voicemail, frowning at her phone, sitting in her dark room. The door to her office was closed. The button beneath her desk activated a buzzer that allowed others entry. The camera over the hall allowed her line-of-sight of anyone attempting to enter.

56

One could never be too careful...

This was partly her reason for distrusting Dakota Steele. The woman was a liability. Agent Carter knew that much.

Steele had quit after a failed case months before. She had a history of chemical dependency. And the report she'd received from Dakota's old supervising agent had been far from "glowing."

Now...

It was strange...

That the same supervising agent was trying to call her.

Especially after how he'd been replaced.

And yet...

She scowled. Fingers now tapping in frustration against her desk.

The phone was ringing again.

Dammit.

She reached out, picking up the device. The man was persistent; she had to give him that at least.

"Yes?" she snapped, answering.

"Agent Carter?" came a rasping, smoke-stained voice.

"Yes," she said. "Drafuss?" She didn't use the term *agent*. She didn't know if it was appropriate. The man was currently in Wit-sec. But also, any time she tried to pry, information was hidden, moved. Former Supervising Agent Drafuss was *not* an easy man to find.

"Carter," Drafuss said, firmly. "You said I ought to call if I needed anything. Well, I need something."

Carter sighed slowly through her nose. "It was meant more rhetorically, Anthony," she said firmly. "It's the polite thing to say when you take a man's job."

Anthony Drafuss coughed on the other line. He cleared his throat. "You're saying you won't help?"

Carter bit her lip. Part of her wanted to flat out refuse... But even though he was no longer an SA... men like Drafuss had a way of making life uncomfortable.

"Call off your dogs, Carter," Drafuss said at last, seemingly deciding on a tone to take. He hadn't chosen to be gentle. A mistake? Or did he know something she didn't.

"What dogs, Anthony?"

"You know... Why is Dakota Steele requesting information on a redacted case? Why am I receiving phone calls from her? And why..." he said, his voice rasping once more, "is she reported to be working for you again? I thought that was handled?"

Carter sighed. "It was. But her partner wanted her back. I made a

57

call."

"I made a call. You agreed. Steele wasn't allowed back."

Carter steepled her fingers now, frowning. "I'm afraid..." she said slowly, taking her time, "that perhaps you must have misunderstood me. Anthony, you are *not* in a negotiating position. I am now in charge of this branch. So maybe it is best you lose this number."

She nodded once, reaching to hang up.

"I'll tell," he said.

She went still.

"Tell what?"

"You know what," he retorted, and she could hear the anger in his voice. It was shaking now. Emotional. Anthony Drafuss had often been a man given to rage. Erratic, out of control. One of the reasons he was no longer sitting in her office. "If you don't tell your hound to quit sniffing around, I'll tell everyone how you bribed your way into the job."

"I did no such thing!" Carter snapped. "I earned this position."

"Yeah? You think your brother's connection to the mayor is gonna be overlooked if I start raising flags?"

Carter snorted. But she paused. She hadn't made it this far by making enemies needlessly. She didn't like being pushed around, but as an authority figure in a chain of command, she knew how to keep rebellion in check. She didn't allow subordinates or superiors to rattle her. Not if she could help it.

So she said, simply, "What are you worried Dakota will find?"

"Nothing. There's nothing. Just tell her to drop it. It's causing headaches. Am I clear?"

Carter considered it. She didn't like Dakota Steele. But she didn't trust or like Anthony Drafuss. She sighed, though, slowly. Then said, simply, "I'll handle it, Anthony. You have my word."

Then she hung up.

CHAPTER THIRTEEN

Darkness came slowly but now covered the sky, hiding the stars and concealing the moon in thick clouds scarcely visible in the nighttime horizon.

Dakota winced, shielding her eyes from the many lights of the crowded section of the city block. Late evening now conceded to night, and Dakota's eyes scanned the windows in the apartment building, attentive and alert. "He's on the first floor," she said, nodding to the lower level.

Marcus scanned the building, his eyes landing on a window with bars covering it. He glanced to Dakota, nodded at the window, then shrugged and stalked forward with lengthy strides.

Dakota followed after, glancing along the sidewalks, beneath the safety lights. Cars continued to swish past along the asphalt road. Pedestrians walking their dogs moved on either side of the street. An old woman was waiting patiently for a bus which was being honked at by a taxi driver.

Dakota and Marcus reached the front door together. Dakota glanced over her shoulder as a woman with a poodle moved past. But the woman didn't turn to enter the apartment, so Dakota returned her attention to the keypad and ran her finger up and down the buzzers.

She then waited patiently. The intercom crackled, but she waited. A few more seconds, then the door buzzed.

"Every time," Marcus murmured. Dakota winked at him. "Which unit again?" he asked, shouldering into the small space.

Dakota came as well, sidestepping a haphazardly placed brown parcel. She scanned the mailboxes and then pointed. "103. There we are," she said, nodding to a number plate a few doors down.

Together, Marcus and Dakota approached.

Dakota shared a look with Marcus, nodding at the door. As she drew closer, she paused, frowning. Loud voices were emanating from inside the apartment unit.

Marcus came to a halt next to her, his hand at his waist. The two of them waited, listening.

Dakota struggled at first to make out exactly what was being said, but she could tell temperatures were getting heated. Then, as the voices grew louder, she picked up the next shouts...

"Too expensive!" a high pitched voice was yelling. "Way too expensive. You can't be serious."

She heard a yelp, the sound of smashing. Then, the same high-pitched voice pleading. "I'm sorry. I didn't know. I'm sorry, I thought it would be cheaper."

Marcus nudged Dakota. She nodded, reached out, and pounded her fist against the door. Marcus's deep, booming voice bellowed, "FBI!"

The voices from inside apartment 103 went quiet. No more sounds of shattering. Dakota shifted, balancing on the balls of her feet. Marcus kept his hand near his holster. Dakota's own hands were curling and uncurling, tapping against her legs.

The silence continued. It was a metal door, so kicking it down wasn't an option. Dakota knocked again. This time, she spoke, and said, "Either you open this door, or we're going to have to call someone who will."

Again, the silence lingered. Dakota heard a muttered protest. She faintly caught someone say, "Did you bring the cops?"

Then the desperate, squeaking voice. "I didn't do anything. This is your fault. It's a set up. You set me up!"

The voices were getting louder again.

Dakota's fist pounded once more. Marcus and Dakota both shouted this time, "FBI. Open the door. Now!"

Dakota could practically feel the air of confusion coming from within the apartment. She waited, listening to some more murmuring. She could feel the uncertainty as they slowly tried to reach a decision. And then, she heard footsteps.

Faint *thumping* steps, a pause. A cleared throat. And then the rattle of the chain on the metal door as it slowly opened.

A giant man, almost as large as Marcus was standing in the gap. He pressed an eye to the door, watching them. The man had a poorly trimmed, patchy beard. His hair was thinning. He wore black clothing, and Dakota immediately noticed he was wearing gloves.

"Hello, sir," Dakota said slowly. "Are you Cleveland Bryant?"

The man shook his head. "Is that the runt's real name?"

Dakota wasn't sure what this meant. "Sir, I'm going to have to ask you to identify yourself."

The man with the patchy beard was glancing between the two agents, sizing them up.

She could feel tremors down her spine now. Marcus shifted on his feet, glaring through the door. "Open up, sir," Marcus snapped.

But the man was now shaking his head. "No, I don't think so."

He tried to shut the door. But Dakota's foot was faster; she caught it.

The man cursed, and tried to slam it.

But this time Marcus shoved with his foot. The sheer size of Agent Clement dislodged the man from bracing against the door. Together, Dakota and Marcus stumbled into the room, through the opening door.

Dakota went still, staring, trying to make sense of the strange scene.

A man was sitting on the couch, shifting nervously and glancing at them. He was handsome, but only a few inches taller than a fifth-grader. He had furtive, darting eyes. He was swallowing, and shifting as the agents stumbled into the room.

The large man in the black outfit with gloves reeled back. But he didn't go far as another figure, also built like a linebacker, caught his comrade. The second man was pale, bald, and shaped a bit like a boulder. Thick fingers, also wearing dark gloves, held his companion from tripping.

This second man was a bit shorter, but also a wider than the first. The two of them were both staring directly at Dakota and Marcus.

The third man, the short one, with the handsome features, sitting on the couch like a schoolchild in timeout, was nursing an injured lip. Blood trickling down the corner of his mouth. Dakota spotted a flowerpot that had been smashed on the ground, dirt scattering. She didn't recognize the flower type.

But she liked flowers. She liked the way they brought life into an otherwise dingy apartment.

She noticed a computer whirring in the background against the far wall, beneath a window with bars next to the machine, there were stacks of books and journals. She noted a corkboard over the whirring computer. Though, it wasn't like any computer she had ever seen. Bright lights flashed from inside a glass case. Even the keyboard was illuminated with red and blue and green.

The apartment smelled faintly of mildew, and aftershave.

The scent of body odor wasn't from the apartment, but rather belonged directly to the two men facing the agents.

Dakota held out a hand, cautioning. "I'm not sure what we stumbled into, here. But I'd like names. Cleveland Bryant?" She said, glancing towards the man on the couch.

He swallowed, squeaked. Yelled, "You brought them here!"

But the two men were also glaring. They shot nasty looks towards the man with the bleeding lip. "Rat. Do you know what we do to rats?"

One of the men reached into his pocket. Marcus began to shout. The man surged towards the small fellow on the couch, pulling a knife from inside his pants.

The second man tried to block the two agents from intervening.

Dakota had a split second to think. She left her gun in its holster.

Fighting, she had faced larger opponents before. In her current line of work, often she was forced to fight men. The benefit of facing a man, was they often overestimated their own abilities compared to hers. In a professional fight, between a martial artist who had trained his whole life, and Dakota, things might have gone differently. But against untrained thugs, who clearly were thinking with their egos, as opposed to brains, things wouldn't be so accommodating. She kicked, hard. Her foot caught the man in the chest, sending him with a shove out of the way.

She hadn't been trying to hurt him, so much as clear a path.

The second man was slashing his knife towards the screaming Cleveland.

She rushed forward. The knife barely missed, as the apartment owner had flung himself to the side in time. The giant shaped like a boulder had stabbed the couch. He ripped his knife, cutting fabric and showering fluff as he aimed for Cleveland a second time.

This time, Dakota hit him from behind, sending him reeling. The man struck the computer desk. The multicolored lights wobbled.

The man snarled, whirling around, knife in hand.

"Drop it!" Marcus shouted. Dakota glimpsed him with his weapon in hand, aiming.

But she knew how much it affected Marcus if he shot someone. Besides, she didn't need it.

She stepped to the right, blocking her partner's line of fire.

Marcus had put himself in danger for her far too many times. She wasn't going to have him risk shooting a second man in as many weeks.

Agent Carter would find a way to blame Dakota, anyway.

Besides, the man clearly didn't know what he was doing with that knife.

He was snarling at Dakota, stalking forward, knife gripped tightly in his hand.

He pointed it at her, and tried to surge forward.

Marcus shouted a warning.

Dakota, had spotted the movement in the reflection of the glass window. The second man, having recovered from her shove, was surging from behind.

As the knife flashed, and the second attacker converged, she moved quickly.

A duck, a punch to the man with the knife. Her fist hit his solar plexus. He let out a sound like a whoopie cushion.

At the same time, she turned, and kicked the man attacking from behind, hard.

Mr. Bryant was screaming from his position on the couch, indifferent to the pain in his bloody lip.

Marcus had cursed, holstered his weapon, and was now charging, following Dakota's lead.

Agent Clement slammed into the man attacking from behind.

Which left Dakota facing the boulder.

The pale, shaved head of the aggressor glared. The knife was still in his hand. He wheezed, gasping from where she had struck him in the chest.

She held out a hand, speaking in as calming a tone as she could muster. "It's going to be okay. Just put down the knife."

"A set up," he snarled. "This was a set up!"

She still wasn't entirely sure what this was all about. But she wasn't in a listening mood either.

The man with the knife surged forward all of a sudden, his blade flashing.

She didn't try to block the hand with the weapon. Instead, she stepped back and to the right, avoiding it entirely. His slash missed. He tried to correct for it, but this affected the speed of the blow. It glanced off the arm of the couch. At the same time, as he rebalanced, bringing his arm back in to stab again, she followed the motion of the blade. When it went forward, she went back. As it went back, she went forward.

A quick dance. Her foot lashed out. She hit the wrist. A loud *crack*.

A scream of pain.

He tried to grip the knife, but his hand wouldn't hold it.

She followed the attack with two punches. Solar plexus, and throat. She wasn't fighting to play fair. She wasn't using octagon rules.

The man gasped, stumbled, dazed and breathless.

He massaged his limp wrist, wincing, letting out a faint whimper of pain.

Dakota pointed directly at him. "Don't move."

But he tried to reach for her with his other hand. So she pushed him, hard. Her foot caught his chest. He stumbled back, tripping over a coffee table covered with strange books.

The man hit the couch, head banging back. He let out a loud exclamation.

Dakota was already reaching for her cuffs.

Marcus was pushing off the second attacker, having handcuffed him on the floor.

Together, they hastened forward to subdue the big man who'd lost his knife.

As they did, mostly with Marcus's help, Dakota's eyes suddenly shifted to the third man in the room.

As the second attacker with the injured wrist was cuffed, she pushed off, breathing heavily, wiping sweat from her forehead. "Mr. Bryant," she said firmly.

He winced, scratching at his chin. "You said you were FBI?" He asked hesitantly. His eyes were glancing towards the two men groaning and wincing and shifting in their handcuffs. They darted back to Dakota and Marcus. He let out another small, deflated squeak.

Dakota pointed a finger at him. "What happened?" she snapped. "What is *this*?"

The small, handsome man had dark hair, long eye-lashes. But he couldn't have been much taller than five foot even. He was still sitting on the couch, exhaling rapidly

Dakota glared directly at Cleveland. The man shifted uncomfortably in his seat, trying to rise, but she pointed at him, and he sunk slowly back onto the couch. His arms spread wide, as if to embrace the air. "I don't know what they were doing here," he began, his voice shaking horribly. His face had gone pale. The blood on his lip was no longer dripping, but had crusted along his chin. He kept shooting nervous glances towards the computer, and towards the coffee table.

Dakota reached out, picking up one of the books. She glanced at the others. "True crime," she said.

The two men, cuffed on the ground, were beginning to rise. But Marcus pushed them both back down. He let out a long exhale, holding them in place.

Dakota trusted her partner to keep them in check. She faced their suspect. "Do you run the online blog *True Novelty*?"

He let out a little squeak of fright. He gave a stuttering response, and shook his head. "I never—I never meant to..."

Dakota didn't speak. Her knuckles throbbed. Her foot was somewhat sore. But she kept her expression impassive.

"I never meant to," he said, more insistently. "It wasn't even my idea. They're the ones who approached me."

"Liar!" shouted the one the size of a small mountain.

Dakota glanced at him. "Approached you about what?"

"Shut up, rat."

But their suspect was no longer scared of the thugs in cuffs. Though he looked downright terrified of Dakota after she had finished pummeling them.

"I don't know what they're talking about. I just—I write stories. It's fun."

Dakota had decided the best tactic with this man was to keep her lips sealed. Sometimes, all a person needed was to dig a little deeper. "It was harmless. Just some brainstorming. There was a movie about it. You know, that one from the '60s."

Dakota just watched.

Now he was shifting uncomfortably, glancing between Marcus and Dakota, swallowing every time he did. He tried to stand up again, but this time Marcus growled, and he lowered back onto the couch. His hands clasped in his lap, trembling. They were as pale as his face now.

"I didn't do anything. I just, wanted to try. It started as harmless fun." The quieter Dakota was the more he seemed interested in talking to fill the space. "Please," he said, stammering, "I'm sorry." Marcus wasn't speaking either. Dakota just watched him. "I didn't mean to." Tears began to slip from his eyes. "It got away from me. I was trying to stop. It was too fun. I don't know why I couldn't stop."

She shared a look with Marcus. He wore a stunned expression. She regarded Cleveland Bryant again.

"I'm sorry," he sobbed, shaking his head hurriedly from side to side. "I'm so, so sorry." He let out a long, shaking sigh.

Again, Marcus and Dakota shared a disbelieving glance.

Marcus cleared his throat hesitantly, then reached slowly for his spare pair of cuffs. Stunned at the confession, Dakota approached Mr. Bryant. "Sir, I'm afraid you're under arrest."

He didn't even look up, as he was still sobbing, shaking his head, and murmuring beneath his breath.

CHAPTER FOURTEEN

Dakota stood across the interrogation room table from where Mr. Bryant was still crying.

Tears traced down his cheeks, and occasionally, he sniffled. Marcus sat across from the man, occasionally handing him tissues from a box that he had grabbed in the break room. Dakota was still puzzling out how this all fit together.

She remained standing, arms crossed and then, clearing her throat, she said. "Mr. Bryant, did you know you were in a room with two known hitmen?"

He looked up at her through red-ringed, bleary eyes. He sniffed and nodded faintly. "Y-yes."

"I see." She glanced at the back of Marcus's head, then up again. "And did you ask to meet them there?"

He sobbed again. "Y-yes... It was just a bit of fun. Just... I know I took it too far..."

Marcus handed the sobbing man another tissue. He shot Dakota a look of confusion, which she returned. They had already run the names and fingerprints of the two large men through their database. Both men were currently in a holding cell, kept in place until they managed to calm down a bit.

"I... I found them online," Cleveland murmured. He sniffed, then used his cuffed hands to blow his nose. "And... And..." he inhaled shakily. "I thought it might work... You know. Like the movies?"

"What movies?" Dakota said. "You keep bringing up movies. You run that blog, don't you?"

"I do..."

"And you've been posting stories about recent murders."

He hesitated, sniffed. "N-no... the blog is fiction. I read true crime, but I write fiction."

Marcus leaned in. "You expect us to believe that you weren't writing about the murders of Billie Childs or Donna Windser?"

He stared at them... "Wh—who?"

Dakota frowned, lifting her phone and, in a clear voice, reciting. *"He came in through the window, watching as she faced the stalls. In one hand, he held the canister, in the other ill-intent..."* She wrinkled her nose. "That doesn't even make sense."

"Hey," he said in a small, hurt voice.

Dakota kept on track. "But," she said firmly, "Stalls? Canister? Come on now... You were describing the murder of Ms. Windser... Except you posted this story three days ago."

He looked back and forth between them, clearly confused. "Are you... *fans?*" he said, his voice hesitant.

Dakota scowled. Marcus leaned in. "Are you attempting to claim it was purely coincidental that the murder this morning nearly exactly matched the story you wrote three days ago?" Marcus made no effort to disguise the disbelief in his voice.

Dakota studied the man across the table. Snot had now mixed with his blood from his busted lip. The tears had left stains along his cheeks. Cleveland shifted uncomfortably, glancing towards the interrogation room door, as if expecting the two large men to come bursting through at any moment.

"It started as a joke," he said, his voice shaky. "The stories were made up. I don't know what you think I did, but, I thought, why were–" he trailed off now, no longer crying, but rather looking quite confused. He glanced between Dakota and Marcus, swallowing hesitantly. He shifted uncomfortably in his chair, and gave a single shrug of one shoulder.

"Maybe you should tell us what you think we arrested you for," Marcus said, slowly.

The man hesitated. "The perfect murder."

Marcus said, "Excuse me?"

"Wait, you mean you're not?" He stiffened, frowning.

Dakota crossed her arms. "What do you mean the perfect murder?"

He wrinkled his nose and shook his head. "I haven't killed anyone. Yet," he said, hesitantly. "Like I said, it was just a joke. Just some fun. But I got carried away. I know that. I shouldn't have done it."

"Done what?" Marcus insisted. "Sir, I'm going to have to ask you to be more clear. If you continue to be coy, we're going to have to end this conversation."

"No, no, wait. I didn't kill anyone. I wasn't going to go through with it. I hired them just to see what the process was like. I'm writing a new book. True crime. The perfect murder."

Dakota tapped her foot against the floor. "Are you saying you were planning to kill someone?"

He shook his head. "Not really. It was just fun. Exciting to think about. I wasn't actually going to go through with it."

Marcus was staring across the table, stunned. Dakota was watching him closely. The tears had stopped, the trembling voice remained the same. He looked a mess, clearly out of his depth. He was shaking as he spoke, like a leaf in a gale.

"It started as a joke on a forum on my website," he said hurriedly, noticing the impatient expressions on the agents' faces. "The idea of a perfect murder. I planned nearly everything. Just for the fun of it. To write about it. I was going to publish it as a book next year. But then it got away from me. I wasn't going to hire those guys to kill anyone. I just wanted to see how much it cost. To see what they could do, what they *would* do."

He swallowed, wetting his throat, and shaking his head again. The man's eyes flashed beneath the bright lights from the ceiling. "I don't have any reason to lie to you. I didn't kill anyone. I didn't have a plan to kill anyone. It was just a joke. I shouldn't have hired them. I shouldn't have taken it as far as I was going with it. But I wasn't actually going to do it."

Dakota noticed how he kept emphasizing this part. Whether she believed him or not, this was not the confession they had been looking for.

She stepped forward now, leaning against the metal table, her hands splayed, her skin touching the cold surface. She said, slowly, "You're saying you didn't kill Billie Childs?"

"No."

"Then how come you are describing their deaths in detail days before the murders?"

He shrugged. "No clue. But it's not me. Maybe the *real* killer is a fan." He seemed to like the thought of this. Quickly, though, he added, "Besides, when were those murders?"

Dakota shot a look at Marcus. He said, wearily, "How about you give us an account of your week, and leave nothing out."

"Easy," he retorted. "Until yesterday, I was in Seattle at a writer's conference. I was on a panel for a few of them for serial stories. You can see the videos online. The stories were written before and are scheduled releases."

Dakota blinked. As far as alibis went, video footage from another state across the country was a pretty good place to start. She said, "Do you have a way to verify that?"

He waved a hand dismissively. "Plane tickets. Online streaming. Videos. Hundreds of people at the conference you can ask. I only got back yesterday."

Dakota glanced at Marcus. If this were true, Bryant would not have been able to attack the first victim. She had a sinking suspicion, studying the man, his alibi would check out. She bit her lip, trying to hold back a frustrated shout.

Marcus was rubbing at his temples. "So you were confessing to *planning* a murder?"

"I thought you came with the hitmen. I thought it was a sting. I didn't know you were there for this."

He looked flabbergasted now, stunned. He shook his head, muttering beneath his breath. Then, slowly, as the full weight of the situation seemed to dawn on him, he lowered his head, resting it in his hands, and letting out a long sigh.

Dakota was already turning, moving towards the door. She was determined to check with the airlines if Cleveland was telling the truth.

But Marcus was sitting there, holding his box of tissues and frowning in the direction of their suspect.

She could see it etched across her partner's face.

Resignation.

Another dead end.

"We're going to have to sort this out with you, sir," said Agent Clement. "Those other two men seemed to think you had detailed schematics for the person you intended to kill."

The man still held his head, but in a small, muted voice, he whispered, "I told them the target's name was Leonardo da Vinci. They asked me if he was an Italian."

Marcus winced. Dakota shoved through the door. She had heard enough.

CHAPTER FIFTEEN

The man walked slowly through the sliding glass doors of the library. He tried his best not to stare too long at any one thing or person. Some of the college students were laughing, checking books out at the counter, or handing their bags to a man behind a desk so he could fill compartments with newly acquired books.

A young woman with bright blue eyes was pointing to a figure through the glass doors at the far wall—the indicated figure was attempting to bicycle down a metal railing over marble stairs.

The wannabe daredevil collapsed in a pile with a faint shout, muffled by the glass. The figures checking out their books rolled their eyes, accepted their returned bags, and headed towards the exit. One of them apologized as his bag accidentally brushed into the chemist.

But the man didn't mind.

These were all specimens to him: strange, interesting, and intricate folk.

He nodded politely, smiling as they filed past through the glass doors.

Then, shouldering his own backpack, he moved through the library, eyes attentive, seeking, searching. He liked libraries. In fact, his favorite, online serial novel had inspired his recent projects. Inspiration came from everywhere if a willing mind was willing to look. But most minds were calloused, putrid things. Stuck in their ten-second videos or thirty-character outrage machines.

He was going to find a new project, and this one would involve a fresh recipe. One of his own

That would keep the police guessing for sure.

He shouldered his backpack strap, fingers taught against the black band.

His other hand gripped the small, metal lunch box. Perhaps not the sort of thing often seen on a college campus, but the perfect size for carrying the thermos inside.

He had spent the better part of a year coming up with this particular concoction.

And now he was excited to share it with others; he could feel faint perspiration along his brow. Could feel his throat tighten as he moved between bookcases and study desks; a few people glanced in his direction. No one recognized him, but it was funny the things people would assume if you had the right props. And in this case, youthful features and the backpack sufficed.

He kept his eyes ahead, occasionally shaking his head briefly.

He moved towards the back of the building, heading in the direction of the study rooms. His eyes darted through the glass windows, skipping from one student to the next. There was a young man arranging notecards on a desk. A woman trying to adjust the pages in a binder.

He moved past, glancing towards a secluded, corner study space. There, in a small room, the door shut, he spotted, through the window, a young woman, frowning as she tried to make sense of a textbook open in front of her. She was wearing headphones.

Perfect. The headphones would distract. The corner room didn't have a window. The perfect place for a test.

He moved forward, stepping behind two rows of bookshelves with science fiction and fantasy as the primary subject matter; he glanced over his shoulder. Line of sight was blocked by the bookshelves.

He slowly lowered the backpack from his shoulder, adjusting his grip. Quietly, he unzipped the main compartment. His fingers found a cold, looping metal item. He flashed a small, nervous smile. This was always the most exciting part. The silence before the storm.

He hastened forward, the bike lock swinging. He reached for the door handle, and wedged the rigid, looping metal lock around the handle, and over the doorjamb, creating something of a barricade.

The lock *clicked* into place. And then, he shot another look back.

One of the students was exiting their study room but didn't glance in the chemist's direction.

He lowered to his knees, and carefully, with trembling fingers, unclasped his lunchbox. He pulled the device from inside. His fingers shaky against the cold metal of the thermos.

He glanced from the top aerosol compartment towards the door.

About half an inch of a gap below the door.

He nodded to himself. Perfect.

He reached into the backpack, pulling out a ghoulish glass and rubber gas mask. He attached a small nozzle onto the end of his thermos.

Over a year of planning. He had created this special.

Now he wore the gas mask. He lodged the nozzle under the door. And then, with a faint, shaky sigh, he pressed the button.

CHAPTER SIXTEEN

Dakota yawned, covering her mouth in the hotel lobby, and watching where Marcus spoke on the phone. A frown curdled his lips. The large man traced a finger along his jaw, shaking his head as he said, "You're sure? Any DNA? *No*?" He sighed, but nodded, lowering his hand, and tapping his fingers against the marble counter. The receptionist was pushing back through an office door, two key cards in hand.

Marcus lowered his phone, glancing at Dakota. "They don't recognize the substance."

She wrinkled her nose, ignoring the look of curiosity on the face of the clerk.

"What does that mean?" she said.

"They're trying to place where it was made but they don't recognize it. It's not like any material they've encountered before."

Dakota let out a faint sigh. She nodded once. "Great," she murmured. "So this guy is coming up with these chemicals on his own."

She trailed off, though, as she glanced at the receptionist, who was extending the key cards to both of them.

She didn't answer the quizzical look on his face. Instead, she nodded once in gratitude, stifled another yawn, and then moved towards the stairs. Marcus waited until they were already halfway up before continuing. "The coroner didn't find anything else. There was no physical interaction between the killer and our victim. No DNA evidence. We double checked the manager's story. The security cameras are for show only."

"So where does that leave us?"

"We're probably going to have to lean heavily into researching the newest victim. See if maybe there's a connection between the victims."

Marcus paused, yawning himself and shaking his head. "Other than that, I can't say."

"Shit."

He nodded adamantly in agreement.

The two of them reached the top of the stairs. Marcus hesitated a moment. He looked at her, flashing a quick, comforting smile. "Are you alright?" he said quietly.

She waved away the concern. "I got heated back there. Just a little re-acclimating. I'm fine."

"No," Marcus said hesitantly. "I mean," he paused, trailed off. He let out a faint sigh.

"No stocked fridges," Dakota said. "I heard you request that. I'm fine, Marcus. I haven't had a drink since I came back."

He looked at her, and he nodded. She could tell, just by looking into his eyes that he believed her. She couldn't say why, but this caused a lump to form in her throat. She coughed, clearing the lump, and shaking her head. She reached out, patting the big man on his bicep.

"I'll be fine. Thank you."

She turned, and began moving down the hall towards her indicated room.

She glanced back. Marcus was still frowning by the banister. He wasn't the sort to be blunt. He often took a more circuitous route when it came to confrontation. She hadn't realized how much she missed him. Hadn't realized how much she wanted to be back with her partner solving cases right alongside him.

She and Marcus had always made a good team.

As she hesitated, key card in her hand, the frail plastic pressed between her fingers, she felt a flash of frustration with herself. Why had she ever thought to quit? Marcus had turned now, moving around the rail, heading in the opposite direction. Agent Clement deserved better. She knew that. She wished she'd considered this last time they'd worked a case together.

Marcus was a friend.

Her best friend. She couldn't imagine what she would do without him.

She smiled after the large man. From behind, it almost looked as if he had bowling balls in his sleeves. She had heard him, when booking the room, asking for the location of the gym.

Some habits were hard to break. And others shouldn't be broken at all.

The light above the door handle flashed green, and she withdrew her key card. She pushed the door open, stepping into the small hotel room. As she did, scanning the single bed, the blinds over a window looking out on the city, and the small side bathroom with fresh towels by the sink, her phone began to ring.

She dropped her key card in surprise. Cursed, bent, picked it up, and then raised her phone. "Yes?"

"Dakota?" It was her father.

She instantly went still. She swallowed, wondering what to say. Their last conversation hadn't gone particularly well.

She hesitated, lowering her laptop onto the bed; she stared out the window, through the cracks in the blinds. "Hey, Dad."

Her father cleared his throat. She rocked uncomfortably back on her feet, slowly lowering onto the bed. She pushed her laptop case aside, and felt the springs creak as she adjusted into a more comfortable position.

For a long moment, silence stretched between the two of them.

For a second, she thought her father had hung up.

But when she raised her phone, and glanced at the screen, it showed the call was still connected.

She let out a breath of air, and then said, "Are you still there?"

"Yeah."

Just like her old man. A single syllable, single word response. She sometimes wondered why she even regretted cutting ties with her father. She had left as a teenager, and never looked back. When her sister had disappeared, all those years ago, her father had thrown himself into investigating the disappearance. He had spent himself, researching everything he could find. He had failed to parent his remaining daughter in his excitement to find his missing one.

She wanted to say she didn't hold it against him.

But that would have been a lie.

Besides, she was confident he held things against her too.

Dakota had been in detention the day her six-year-old sister had been taken. Dakota was supposed to walk her sister home from school. But due to the afterschool discipline, Carol had walked home alone.

All they had found was a backpack with a streak of blood.

These memories soured in her mind as she shifted uncomfortably on the hotel bed

"You don't need money, do you?" he said at last.

"Excuse me?"

"I was just trying to think why you're calling."

Her hand bunched around the phone, tight. She resisted the urge to throw the device across the room.

"No," she said, testily. "I'm not looking for money, Dad. I wanted to touch base."

She swallowed. Again, he didn't reply.

"I was wondering," she said, slowly, "if maybe I could get a look at that red folder."

74

"Right, so you said. What do you think you can do with it?"

Dakota exhaled slowly. "In my position, Dad, I have resources that could help."

Her father didn't respond. He was doing this a lot, now.

"Dad," she said quietly.

"Yeah?"

"Maybe, maybe I should–" she cut herself off, biting her lip. Did she really want to apologize? It had been a long time since they had spoken. He probably blamed her.

But he had been absent for nearly five years before she left, and before that, he hadn't exactly been father of the year anyway.

Carol would not have had to walk home, even with Dakota in detention, if her father hadn't been drunk at the time.

She felt a flare of familiar resentment.

"Shit," he muttered. "Not sure what you want from me."

"I'm not looking for anything. I just want those notes."

"Want me to read them?"

She wasn't sure if he was being sarcastic. "Why don't you scan them?"

"Right, right. I mean, there's a lot. Why don't you give me a little bit of time to think about it. You're not nearby, are you?"

She let out a faint sigh. She was pretty confident she had already told him this. But she said, in as polite a tone as she could muster, "I'm in Arizona right now, Dad. I'm working out of Virginia."

"Yeah. You said. All right. Virginia. Okay." His voice was devoid of emotion. "Good luck," he said quietly.

And then her father hung up.

She wasn't surprised at this point. It wasn't like the two of them particularly wanted to spend time together. Wasn't like she even knew where to start speaking with her old man.

She let out a long sigh, and flopped on the bed. She stared at the ceiling, and only paused to shoot a glance towards the lock on the door, making sure it was shut.

She wasn't sure of the path forward. But she knew one thing was certain.

If anyone had new information on her sister's disappearance, it would be her father.

And additionally, she realized, while they were currently at a dead end in their case, nothing beat regular police work. They would have to make some calls the next day. Have to follow the evidence where it led. No matter what, she wasn't going to let the killer get away with it.

Not the way The Watcher had escaped four months ago, targeting women. Not the way the bastard who had killed Carol had done, twenty years ago.

The reason she hunted them. The reason she didn't let them escape, was to provide for others a proper end to a story which she had never received herself.

CHAPTER SEVENTEEN

Dakota yawned, trying her best to keep her eyes from drooping over the small, round breakfast table in the back of the lounge. The hotel breakfast bar was mostly empty. Dakota watched as Marcus made a second trip to the coffee maker, skirting pointedly past the bagels which looked a few days too old.

As he returned and sat at the small table, he said, "Did you get my message?"

Dakota glanced at her phone, but nodded. "Saw it when I woke up. So what's that connection?"

Marcus settled in the chair, which was far too small for him, and leaned forward, using his large elbows to prop himself up.

"I think," he said, firmly, "I've found the connection between the victims. Remember how her coworkers mentioned Ms. Childs was a grad student?"

Dakota nodded.

"Well, it turns out our first victim worked in an admissions office at a local college."

Dakota perked up. She spun a silver spoon through a bowl of corn flakes, watching as the milk sloshed. "Let's say that is the connection. Our third victim, Donna, wasn't in college."

"Right," he said, frowning and leaning back. "She's a high school student."

"Was. She just graduated."

"Maybe it has something to do with graduation."

Dakota shrugged. "But our first victim is involved in an admission's office. That seems like a stretch."

Marcus took a sip from his coffee, the steam wafting up past his cheeks. He said, slowly, "Maybe," he paused, biting his lip, "maybe we should check and see if Donna was accepted into any universities... It could help us narrow down who the killer is targeting. Also, I've been thinking about Mr. Bryant's online novel. What if the killer really is using some of the stories as a blueprint? Think we could find him that way?"

Dakota checked digital clock on her phone. "Could take ages to sort through tens of thousands of visitors. Besides, most people use VPNs nowadays. Let's try the family."

It was still early. A bit before seven a.m. Then again, usually, in her experience, the surviving family members of the victim were more than willing to talk to the police.

Marcus pointed a finger at her, nodding as he did. He reached towards his phone, his brow lowering as he cycled through their most recent emails, studying the victim profile for Donna Windser.

"Margaret Windser," Marcus said quietly. "She lived alone with her mother."

Dakota sighed. "Not going to be a fun conversation. Want me to take it?"

Marcus shifted uncomfortably, staring at his phone, the white glow illuminating his dark knuckles. He sighed at last, though, and said, "No... no—I can do it. Think she'll be up?"

"She'll be up," Dakota said. She remembered when her sister had vanished. Her father hadn't slept for days.

Marcus raised his phone, and Dakota took another bite of the soggy cereal. She didn't use too much milk. The taste of honey and corn residue in the bottom of the cereal bowl reminded her too much of the flavor of mead.

It was strange, the odd things that triggered a bad habit. Dakota, swallowed her mouthful of breakfast food, then watched as Marcus frowned.

He shook his head towards Dakota, shrugging but keeping the phone to his cheek. "She's not answ—oh, hello, Mrs. Windser?"

Marcus lowered the phone flat, holding it in the air with the speaker on so Dakota could hear.

"Y—yes?" said a muffled voice. "Who is this, please?"

"My name is Agent Clement," Marcus said. "You're on the line with my partner Agent Steele. Do you have a moment, Mrs. Windser?"

"Miss."

"Oh, sorry. Ms. Windser."

A long, deflated sigh. A yawn. Dakota could picture the bleary eyes, the weary, haggard expression, though she'd never met the woman.

"I suppose... I already spoke with a policeman yesterday."

"I'm aware," Marcus said quickly. "And I'm very thankful for your help. Just..." He bit his lip. "I was wondering if you could tell us about Donna's scholastic aspirations."

"Excuse me?"

"Was Donna applying to colleges?" Dakota said firmly.

"Umm... She only..." A swallow, a long—too long pause—

suggesting the mother was gathering herself. When she spoke again, her voice was clipped. "She only just graduated high school." A sniff. "She was going to take a gap year."

"I see," Dakota said, frowning.

Marcus let out a faint sigh of frustration. He said, "Thank you for your time, Ms. Windser."

"Wait," she said. "Why? Is that important? Was it someone from my school?"

Dakota perked. "Your school, ma'am?"

"I—yes... I work at a community college here."

Dakota and Marcus both leaned forward now, staring at the phone. "In what capacity?" Dakota said, her throat dry all of a sudden.

"Admissions counselor... my job didn't have anything to do with it, did it?"

"Which school?" Dakota asked, seamlessly avoiding the question.

"I've been at a couple. I'm now working for Tampa Tech. Why? Please... please tell me *something.*" Her voice cracked.

Dakota shot Marcus a look. Her partner said, quietly, his voice soothing, "Ma'am. I promise you, we're doing everything possible. And I just want to say, I admire the daughter you raised. You did something *very* special." Marcus sighed slowly, his voice shaking with emotion. Dakota wasn't sure how her partner was able to do this. To empathize so easily. She admired him for it, though it was a foreign concept to her. "And I must add," he said, "that what has happened is unfair. I promise to do everything to bring you justice."

A voice crack, another small sob. No words this time, but Marcus didn't bid farewell. He just kept the phone raised, listening as Ms. Windser cried in the background.

Dakota pushed from her chair, moving hastily towards the breakfast cereal bar. She didn't want seconds, but she couldn't sit by and listen.

The tears... they bothered her. She could remember her father's own tears. Remember what it had done to her family.

She could only hope that Ms. Windser had others in her life. People who would come alongside and help her.

A killer who targeted young women didn't just take a single life— he affected many others.

She sighed, standing, facing the tall plastic chutes of breakfast cereal, her bowl clutched in one hand. She tried not to listen as Marcus finished speaking, her own mind returning to the case.

She didn't have Clement's soothing manner. Didn't have the ability to empathize on a dime.

But she caught killers.

She brought people to justice and put men behind bars who couldn't be trusted to exist in the broader society.

She paused and waited until she heard Marcus clearing his throat from behind her. She turned swiftly now, facing her partner.

"Well?" he said, watching. His phone was lowered. "Three of them have connections to local colleges."

"Different colleges," Dakota pointed out.

"Still..."

She nodded slowly, the cereal bowl tapping against the plastic counter. She let out a faint sigh, inhaling the scent of stale bagels and coffee.

"Maybe... maybe we need to check the local colleges for anything untoward... The killer only just started last week. Maybe something happened."

Marcus was nodding. "Some inciting incident. Good call. Alright. Anything to narrow it down?"

Now, though, Dakota was clicking her fingers, marching back towards where her laptop bag rested against the chair legs. "Yes, in fact. I want to look up any criminal incidents involving laboratories or chemicals at colleges in a fifty mile radius. How about you call the universities and see if anyone faced internal disciplinary measures."

Dakota and Marcus both nodded at each other, sitting right back down at the table.

A man, wearing a bathrobe had appeared in the door, but got one look at their expressions and, after snatching a banana and muttering a quick "'morning," retreated to safer pastures.

Dakota was already pulling her computer out, setting it on the surface of her black, laptop bag and quickly entering her password. She heard Marcus's phone ringing across from her as he placed the first of his calls.

She focused, though, staring at the screen as she completed the two-factor authentication with her phone and entered one of their main databases. Criminal complaints and arrests could often be researched through local record portals, even using keywords now.

So she did, tapping away, frowning as she did, feeling a slow prickle of excitement.

Another lead.

She felt like a bloodhound with a scent.

Another lead meant another shot at catching this bastard.

She entered, *"chemical lab,"* or, *"chemistry,"* or, *"chemical attack.*"

She tried a variety of word combinations, then narrowed the parameters into a fifty mile radius around the previous three murders. The latest had been on the border, but still within the same distance as the first two. She also limited the research to college campuses, both local and state.

And then...

She hit enter.

Her eyes darted along the screen, gathering information as the results were hastily displayed. She scanned quickly, studying the information as best she could as it rolled out like a hastily unfurled carpet.

"Come on..." she muttered.

Marcus was talking now, but she ignored this.

The search results finally appeared. She made sure to narrow the results by a single-year parameter.

And then she went stiff, wrinkling her nose.

She double-checked, but felt a faint flicker of frustration.

There were nearly twenty pages of results. Over fifteen results per page.

She let out a faint sigh, hunching in her chair now, and feeling a slow, dawning sense of resignation.

There went her morning.

Then again, it would take Marcus some time to complete his calls anyway.

This was what she'd decided to do after all, wasn't it? Follow the evidence wherever it led.

Evidence was king.

And so she straightened her posture, adjusting the edges of her long-sleeved shirt and clicked the first link, tabbing it into another window. She did it with all of the results on the first page. And, determinedly, exhausted, she began to read.

***

Dakota was yawning again as she deleted one of the results from her search page. Only five left... So far, most of the incidents had involved theft. Objects being stolen or broken... A few vandalism. One sexual harassment. And another—an illicit, but legal, affair between a professor and a grad student. This last one had been filed as a report but redacted.

81

She shook her head, trying to maintain her focus. She glanced at the small clock in the corner of her computer, feeling a sense of lethargy. Nearly quarter past noon.

The morning had disappeared. Her eyes stung. The small, morning breakfast lounge had been cleared. Occasionally she heard laughter, or the sound of footsteps on the other side of the hall, tinged with the scent of chlorine and gusts of warm, humid air.

She shook her head, refocusing.

Another result...

Someone had made racial comments to a professor. She shook her head, deleting this result as well.

It didn't fit the profile.

She moved onto the next.

Marcus had lowered his phone, finally, and was frowning at her. When he spoke, his voice was hoarse from overuse. "Anything?" he said.

She hesitated. "You?"

He shook his head. "Twenty schools in the parameters provided. Two didn't pick up the phone. Two refused to speak without a warrant. But the others either didn't know of any incident that matched my question, or didn't have any familiarity with the victims."

Dakota winced but nodded. She deleted another search result.

Three left.

"How about you?" he said in that same hoarse, overused voice.

She sighed, leaning back and shaking her head. "I... I can't be sure," she murmured. "Umm... Nope." Another deleted one.

Two results left. She opened the second to last... Read through the report. And then her eyebrows shot up.

"What is it?"

Dakota re-read the file. She moved to the last result just to be sure—but no. The last result was a vandalism report.

She shook her head, deleted it, and returned to the previous result. She realized why it had been displayed in the final page of results. It had been pursued as a civil case, not criminal. But the report had started as criminal.

She re-read the information.

"What?" Marcus pressed.

"This one," Dakota said, tapping a finger. "From College of Lepage. There was an associate professor with something of a sexist streak. A Professor Burke."

"And what's eye-catching about Prof. Burke?"

82

"Well..." Dakota glanced down the report towards the later information. "He was fired for a demonstration that burned a student's hand."

Marcus perked up. "Excuse me?"

"It looks like some of the other students thought it was intentional. But Burke claimed it was a demonstration gone wrong. One of his own little concoctions. But the student who's hand he burned, accidentally, according to him, had reported him two weeks prior for inappropriate comments to a female student. Some of the faculty thought it was reprisal as well."

Marcus was now standing, phone back in his pocket as if loathe to see the device again. "So let me get this straight—a professor at a community college creates some chemical concoction and uses it allegedly to burn the hand of a student who reported him two weeks prior? Our first victim had applied to this school, right?"

Dakota looked up, having committed the subsequent portion to memory. "Yes—that's a connecting point, but also according to Burke, the chemical demonstration was one he'd done previously. It was an accident, he says."

"Right... Criminal charges?"

"None. He was fired, though. And... yes, so in civil court the college paid out some undisclosed sum in settlement to the student."

Dakota frowned. She went back to the same search bar, but this time entered the social security number of Edmund Burke. She waited a moment, and then her eyebrows shot up. "Hang on," she said. "I have something else. Our ex-professor sent a threatening letter to his school. Nothing actionable, but he apparently used phrases like 'Explosive reprisal.' And, how he didn't mean to 'Bomb in class.'"

"So using euphemisms to make a threat. This was *after* he was fired?"

"Exactly."

"So where is Mr. Burke working now?"

Dakota tapped her finger against the back of her keyboard, accidentally lowering the volume. She followed the link to Mr. Burke's tax information from the IRS. She scanned down to his employer form, then her eyes shot up. "Unemployed, but he's still living in the same community. Looks like our professor comes from money. Place called Meadow Oaks."

Marcus wrinkled his nose. "Didn't realize professors were paid so much."

"Yes... well, the house is listed on Zillow for nearly two million."

83

"Huh. The guy didn't start cooking meth in the off-season, did he?" Marcus quipped.

"I think I've seen that show," Dakota muttered. "But no... looks like the house was his brother's."

"Was?"

"We can ask him about it when we get there. You good driving?" Dakota had pushed to her feet and was already closing her laptop, slipping it into the case.

Marcus flashed a thumbs up and was already slipping around the table, moving towards the door. Another gust of chlorine-tinged, moist air wafted into the room from the direction of the hotel swimming pool.

Marcus and Dakota hastened, together, out the front doors.

CHAPTER EIGHTEEN

Dakota's fingers tapped impatiently against the side of their sedan, her arm extended through the window, the edge of one of her tattoos displayed beneath the hem of her sleeve.

The guard sitting in the cubicle behind the gate to Meadow Oaks frowned at the two agents, glancing towards a clipboard, then back up at them, his dark scowl peering between the metal bars.

"I don't see an appointment with Mr. Burke," he said.

Dakota bit her lip, fingers tap-tap-tapping.

Marcus shook his head. He said, "Well, sir, please take another look at—"

"No, I saw your badge." the guard replied, scratching at pale hair with a gnarled finger. "But that doesn't change my job. FBI or not, this is a private community."

Marcus, ever patient, continued. "I understand sir. I realize we're putting you in a difficult position, but—"

Dakota blurted out. "We'll blockade both sides of the street and then tell all the neighbors that it's because *you* Jerome, wouldn't let us do our job. How about that?"

Marcus looked slowly at her, then sighed. Dakota winced, realizing how harsh she'd sounded.

But Jerome hesitated, scratching at his nametag. "I..." he frowned back at his clipboard. "Mr. Burke," Dakota repeated, firmly.

The guard tapped a pen against his lips. Then said, "12 Willow Street? Ah... right..." He frowned, white eyebrows darting low. "No Christmas tip from that address." He looked up and shrugged. Then, without another word, he tapped a button behind his glass cubicle. The gates slowly began to open.

Marcus let out a long breath which he'd apparently been holding.

Dakota resisted the urge to apologize for strong-arming the gate guard. Marcus had his methods; she had hers.

It was best she didn't confuse the two.

They trundled up the smooth, black asphalt. Even the roads were well-maintained, lined by hedges and flowers in freshly mulched beds. Ahead, she spotted large homes surrounding manufactured lakes. Pristine grass, clean water, fountain spray sparkling on the air, catching the sunlight and cast rainbows across the lakes.

The homes were all large, five thousand square foot minimum, mostly of stone with intricate facades displaying artistry in the form of arches and half-columns and occasional trellises over gazebos laden with ivy.

Marcus moseyed along the path, moving slowly, glancing at the street names and house numbers. He didn't look nearly so impressed by the buildings or the landscapes.

Dakota was pretty sure some of the houses were bigger than the public school she'd attended twenty years ago. "Wow," she murmured, staring at a building that stretched over half an acre in every direction, with more wings and attached garages and large patios than Dakota had ever seen.

Marcus noted her attention. He nodded politely. "Very pretty," he said.

Dakota just shrugged. She supposed Clement had come from money, so these sorts of things were more commonplace.

But Dakota, growing up as she had, could remember days— especially when hanging with the wrong crowd—where they would go for joy rides and occasionally drive through the rich neighborhoods, staring enviously at the buildings.

Occasionally, one of the members of the group would walk up to the houses at night, peering through the windows.

Dakota had never done anything but look, but she could remember a floor-to-ceiling aquarium she'd once seen through a bay window.

"There we are," Marcus said, pointing.

She noted a silver sign that read *Willow*.

Now, they moved along the street, rolling past more large homes. At the end of the cul-de-sac, though, Marcus pulled to a halt. A long driveway ended in a sleek, blue and black mailbox with a flag shaped like a pennant. A bright, golden number *12* ornamented the box.

"Looks like our gate guard might have called ahead," Dakota muttered, nodding and pointing through the window.

Marcus peered out and went still, frowning towards where a man was staring at them from over a white, marble railing around a second-floor terrace.

The man stared down at them, glaring, his hands spread, resting in the green ivy tangled across the top of the rail.

"Huh," Dakota murmured. "He doesn't look happy."

Marcus pulled slowly up the driveway, came to a halt, and with Dakota, pushed out of the doors, frowning towards the patio. The big man raised a hand and gave a little wave. "Mr. Burke?" Marcus called out.

"Professor!" the man on the patio snapped back, still glaring.

His hair was combed back into a dark pony-tail. The hue didn't quite match his age. He had wrinkles around his eyes, and an upturned nose hinting at some sort of cosmetic work.

He was fidgeting constantly with a small, black shoe-polish goatee. He looked nervous, too.

"He definitely knows who we are," Dakota murmured beneath her breath.

Marcus nodded nearly imperceptibly. He called out, a bit louder, "I'm Agent Clement. This is Agent Steele. We'd like to speak with you, Professor Burke."

But the man was shaking his head. "Go away!" he called, his voice strangled. "Get out of here. It's private property."

Dakota who was getting somewhat tired by the obstacles, stepped around the hood of the car. Her expression was impassive, emotionless. Her tone dull as she said. "Sir, we need to speak with you. We can do that down here in the driveway or at a station. Your choice."

"That isn't much of a choice!" he retorted.

Dakota supposed he had them there. It wasn't much of one. She sighed, opened her mouth to speak again as she took another few steps up the smooth driveway.

As she did, though, the man held out a hand and yelled. "Go away! This isn't fair—it isn't! You shouldn't be here. Hasn't cruelty taken enough from me!" he yelled at them. His face was red. Only then did Dakota notice the nearly empty wineglass by his hand.

She wondered if the bottle was similarly deprived.

"Sir!" she called. "How about you come down from there and tell us yourself? Is that the front door? We can meet you there!" She waved towards a giant set of doors lined by marble lions.

But the man was shaking his head. "The door isn't locked!" he snapped. "Come in if you want. Come into this sinking ship. This cursed reality. What you see before you, dangling over these vines is a wretch! And you are his persecutors!"

Marcus glanced at Dakota. Dakota shook her head. The monologuer—the worst type of drunk.

She tried to interrupt, but now he was pontificating by waving a finger around, his shoe-polish goatee jutting out, his pony-tail swishing side to side, the wrinkles around his eyes narrowing in rage.

"My brother's home, this. He died too! Killed by fate..."

Dakota noticed the word *too.* She tensed now, frowning, hand near her holster. She moved further up the driveway, Marcus in tow.

"Sir!" she said quietly, "how about you sit down? We can come to you!"

"No!" he screamed at them. And he flung his wine glass. It only made it a couple of feet, smashing against the ground, uselessly.

Dakota and Marcus had both gone still, tensed, facing the ivy-tangled porch.

But Mr. Burke had now spun on his heel, shouting incoherently, waving a hand over his head as if bidding farewell and marching back into his mansion.

"He said *too,*" Dakota muttered quickly.

"I heard him. Door's unlocked! Go!"

Dakota hastened forward, towards the half open door. Marcus broke into a sprint. Dakota shoved through first, shoulder into the metal frame.

The door didn't creak so much as glide smoothly open.

Marcus and Dakota stumbled into the hall, eyes wide.

And that's when the scent struck her...

Fumes...

Her eyes widened.

Gasoline.

"Shit!" Dakota cursed. "Look!"

A figure had rushed down a set of stairs and stumbled into an adjoining room. She watched a flash of blue, silk slippers as the figure spun around, shouting still.

Dakota and Marcus both had weapons drawn now, but pointed to the floor. Slowly, they approached the door.

Mr. Burke was standing in what looked to be a library, surrounded by shelves of books. "Ha!" Burke exclaimed. "Aha! Aha! My own home! I die in my own home, too!"

The stench of gasoline now flooded the air, spilling from inside the library. Dakota spotted the red canister first, toppled on the ground.

"Guard warned him," Marcus muttered. "He's drenched the place."

Dakota noticed the toppled books, the stains in the carpet. The gasoline had been poured everywhere. And now, she noted the small, green plastic item in Mr. Burke's hand. He held it up, eyes blazing, teeth set tightly, lips curled back like a snarling hound.

"Sir, don't!" Dakota yelled. "Don't do it—wait!"

Marcus noticed the lighter a split second later.

They both had frozen. Dakota, though, slowly, began edging

forward again. She didn't know what to say, how to keep him from immolating himself.

Thankfully, Marcus began to speak. He lingered back—not out of fear, she knew. He was protective of her. But because, like her, Marcus knew he was the more intimidating presence. Giant-sized, muscled, male... Men would often react differently to him than to Dakota.

So Dakota moved forward while Marcus lingered back, speaking in that same soothing voice he'd used on the phone.

"Sir," Marcus said, slowly, eyes on their suspect. "Could you consider this for a moment, please? We don't want to see you hurt yourself."

Dakota took another step forward.

Mr. Burke's eyes darted from her to Marcus then back. He swallowed briefly, shaking his head furiously. "No point," he whispered. "There's no point... What's the point?"

Marcus said something else, but Dakota was no longer paying attention. Her eyes were fixed on the man's finger pressing to the lighter.

She took another step. He tensed.

She paused.

Marcus said something. The man relaxed a bit.

She took another step. She was only a few feet away now. He stood just inside the glass doors leading to the gasoline-drenched library.

"You don't really want to do this," Marcus was saying, softly.

Dakota inched forward again.

But Mr. Burke froze. He glanced at her. His eyes widened in horror as if realizing how close she really was.

Then, with a snarl, he exclaimed, "Goodbye!" And he shoved the lighter towards the ground, closer to the fumes as he flicked it.

CHAPTER NINETEEN

Dakota didn't hesitate. She darted forward, closing the distance. Mr. Burke screamed in rage, but as he flicked the lighter, her foot shot out—she had always been known for her kicks back in her fighting days.

Before he could set the room ablaze, her foot connected with the lighter. He yelled, his hand flinging back. The small, plastic device spun through the air. At the same time, Marcus burst forward. Burke stumbled, sobbing as he tried to catch the lighter. But it was far from his grasp. It hit the carpet harmlessly. He tried to lunge at it. But Marcus had reached him now. A large hand closed around the disgraced professor's wrist, holding him tight.

Dakota was breathing heavily, feeling a flush along her cheeks. She knew that had been risky.

Marcus was busy guiding Mr. Burke out of his library. "Sir, please. Stop resisting." Marcus was pulling his handcuffs from behind his back.

There seemed to almost be an air of reluctance as he did it. She didn't fault the big man. Somewhere between empathy and their job, Marcus had his own battles to fight. Now, shakily, wincing against the stinging odor of gasoline, Dakota glanced at the small lighter resting on the floor. She shook her head, and pulled her phone from her pocket. Hastily, she dialed emergency services.

And then, with quick motions, she followed Marcus back out the front door towards fresh air.

***

Dakota could still smell gasoline on her clothing. She could still feel the way her body had moved, her foot connecting with Mr. Burke's hand. She was glad she wasn't still in the large mansion that had been prepared to go up in flames. Thankfully, the fire department had arrived in time to neutralize the gasoline and dispose of the lighter. Occasionally she glanced at her phone, watching as she received updates from the emergency response teams.

No one harmed. Nothing burned. At least there was that.

Now, Agent Clement was sitting on the same side of the interrogation table as their suspect. He had a chummy, open air about him. Marcus rested his hands on the table, and was leaning towards Burke, saying, "Maybe I'm reading this wrong. But, if you look at this line, it does sound like you're threatening to blow up the school."

Dakota was sitting on the other side of the table, watching the two of them; she wasn't sure where Agent Clement's comforting line of questioning would lead but she was content to wait, to watch. Burke still had tears streaking his face. He shook his head, handcuffs scraping against the table. "It isn't like that," he insisted. "I was using hyperbole for rhetoric. That was all."

"I see," Marcus said. "Because to me, if I'm honest, it looks like you were frustrated. Maybe even scared, and you wanted the school to be scared as well."

The man glared at Marcus. "Maybe," he replied. "What do you know about it?"

"We know you were fired," Dakota interjected, leaning across the table and watching their suspect. "We know you made overtures toward some of your female students. We know you burned a student's hand."

"Accident." He scowled at her now.

"And was it an accident what we just witnessed back at your house?"

"That was a foregone conclusion. Not my fault."

Dakota crossed her arms, glaring, her feet set against the floor with the same rigidity as the metal chair. "It never is your fault, is it?" she said firmly. "Everyone else is to blame, except for you. Isn't that right?"

He stared at her. "I was doing fine. I was a good teacher. Ask anyone."

"The faculty doesn't seem to think so. The students didn't think so."

"A conspiracy. Jealous sorts who wanted my job. That was all."

Dakota shook her head, frowning. "I don't know what it is to live with that much delusion, sir. But regardless, I've read that email too. You mentioned you were going to bomb the classroom."

He snorted. "I mentioned that I bombed in the classroom. It's a euphemism for–"

"I know what it's a euphemism for. But that's not what you meant."

"What do you need me here for? You seem to have convinced yourself."

Dakota rubbed at her nose, and shot a look at Marcus.

He cleared his throat, and leaned back. "Sir, I need to ask you where you were yesterday."

"Why?" He frowned, his tone more alert all of a sudden. He glanced between the two of them, his eyes darting back and forth. "What is this about?" he said, more insistently. "What do you think I did?"

Dakota shot Marcus a look. He returned it. Mr. Burke said, "Did something happen at the school?" He let out a long sigh. "A *bomb*? Is that what this is about?"

"Do you know Billie Childs?" Dakota said, keeping them on track.

He shrugged. "Never heard of her. Was that a student of mine?"

Dakota said, "Would you have remembered if she was a student?"

He was shaking his head again, though, resting his hands flat against the table, the handcuffs tilted across his wrists, pointing towards her.

"Sir," Marcus said, slowly, "How about Donna Windser? Does that name ring any bells?"

But the last two victims didn't register.

Dakota could see his blank expression. Still, this was potentially a product of him choosing random victims. She didn't know that he knew their names. Or perhaps he had simply forgotten them in his drunken, unstable stupor.

He said, "The murder victims?"

She perked up.

Marcus said, "So you do know them?"

"Of course. Seeing as I killed them."

He was now leaning back in his chair. If anything, he looked smug.

"You're saying you *did* kill them?" Dakota said, frowning.

He wagged his head firmly. "Of course I did. Who else? I killed them. Actually, I think I killed more than them."

Dakota hesitated. There had been another victim. But she couldn't tell now. Was he fishing? Was he playing with them? She wasn't sure why, but even in his confession, she didn't feel as if Mr. Burke was being honest with them. So she said, "How about you start from the beginning?"

But he smacked his lips, and leaned back. "I'm bored. Why don't you let me go back to my cell?"

"We haven't put you in a cell yet," Marcus said.

"No, but I know you have one waiting for me. And I don't have anything else to say. I'm not sorry I did it. I killed them. I had fun."

Dakota was confused. One moment he'd been sobbing, waxing poetic about how unfair the world was. And now here he was, admitting to it. As if he had done a one-eighty.

She shook her head, and said, "What can you tell us about the women you killed?"

He looked at her, and shrugged a single shoulder. "It was fun."

"And how did you do it?" Dakota said, firmly.

The man met her gaze, also glaring.

Marcus was glancing between the two of them.

Mr. Burke cleared his throat, his tongue darting out and wetting his lips. Then, quickly, he said, "An explosion. Just like it says in the letter. Why else would you think it was me?"

Dakota didn't blink. She didn't betray anything in her expression. But she felt a flash of frustration.

The first victim, like the last two had been killed with chemicals. Aerosol and tranquilizer.

No explosions.

So why was he lying? And what was he lying about?

Had he killed them, and was he now trying to throw them off the scent?

He had been ready to set himself on fire. It wasn't like this man was super interested in self-preservation.

Dakota felt a jolt of frustration. She also felt guilt. She didn't have sympathy for the man. Part of her wanted to, but another part of her couldn't forget the sobbing mother on the phone call at breakfast.

"Sir," she said, slowly, "how many women did you kill?"

He shrugged. "Only three."

This part was correct. Again, she felt confused. Was he admitting to crimes he had committed? The method, though, he was making up. Unless, of course, he had seen something on the news. It was possible he didn't know the full extent of the case. Perhaps he was only admitting to what he knew about.

He shook his head, and said, firmly, "What more do you need from me? I did it. I've admitted to it. So how about we move this along? I don't want a lawyer. I'll represent myself."

Marcus shook his head. "Hang on, you're getting ahead of yourself. How about you help us out. What were the names of your victims?"

He shook his head. "I don't know."

Dakota frowned. "And what did they look like?"

He said, "They were women. What else is there to know?"

She glanced at Marcus. He returned the look. She could see the doubt in his eyes as well. Both of them, she realized, weren't buying it.

Mr. Burke was lying. At least, lying about some things. So how had he known there were three victims?

"Burke," she said slowly, "what news station do you use?"

He glanced at her, sharply, but then looked away just as quickly. He shrugged nonchalantly. "I don't really watch the news."

Marcus said, "And these crimes," he said, "The ones from last month—why did you stop?"

Mr. Burke hesitated. He looked confused. He said, "They weren't from last month. The last murder was three days ago."

Again, partially true and partially not. They hadn't yet reported the murders of Donna or Ms. Childs to the news. Of course, people had seen the spectacle at the gas station. But the reality behind it hadn't yet been revealed. At least the gas station attendant had been told to keep his lips shut.

But now, her mind was spinning. Why was Mr. Burke saying these things? Was he lying on purpose?

As she stared at the man, his face tinged red from his drink, she wasn't so sure.

Marcus was frowning skeptically. Clearly, he wasn't convinced that they had their man. His next question confirmed this suspicion, "And so these bombs you used, how did you make them?"

Burke excitedly launched into a complicated discussion of all the ways he had crafted his explosives.

Dakota wasn't listening, though. She was watching. Watching his physical reactions to the questions. Sometimes excited, other times scared. A twitch of an eye, a faint fidget. The sound of a swallow.

It all mattered. It could all be read.

Now, though, her mind was getting heavy. She could feel the weight of her choices.

Burke was lying, but was he the killer?

Her phone began to ring.

She frowned, glancing towards Burke. He watched her curiously, and said, "You should probably answer that."

She scowled at him, pushed from her chair and turned to face the wall, shouldering the phone and speaking softly. "Hello?"

"Is this Agent Steele?" came the reply. It was Marsters. The Homeland Security agent from the gas station.

"Is everything all right?"

"I'm afraid we have another victim. They found her an hour ago. She's currently still at the crime scene. I wanted to give you a chance to get over here before moving her."

Dakota closed her eyes, and exhaled faintly.

"Where are you?"

"The University. It's about an hour away from the city. Here, I can text you the address."

Marsters hung up. But a second later her phone buzzed with a message.

She stared at it, and looked back up at Mr. Burke.

The address was nearly two hours away from where he lived.

Was he lying? Or now trying to play insane in order to make them think that he was innocent?

She shook her head in frustration but gestured towards Marcus.

"Let's go," she said.

The big man looked over. "Is everything okay?"

"We need to go," she said, more insistently.

He nodded hurriedly, pushed from the table, without a glance back. Dakota looked at their suspect. She said, "A sergeant will be in to check on you. Why don't you provide him your report the same way you did us."

He sneered at her. But she turned away, indifferent to his approval.

As she picked up the pace, Marcus followed her out of the interrogation room and into the hall. "What happened?" he said, frowning.

"Another body," she replied.

Marcus grimaced. Dakota shook her head. "It's about an hour from here—so another forty minutes from his place. Either Mr. Burke is a fast driver, and we got to him after he returned, or he's full of shit."

Marcus nodded once, his shoes squeaking against the tile floor. "He didn't seem like the most reliable witness. Even while confessing."

"Yeah, I didn't think so either. It was like he did a one-eighty. Like he realized what we were after and wanted to confess, though I don't know why."

"He's not exactly interested in preserving himself right now," Marcus said with a sigh. "We should send someone back there with him."

Dakota was already moving towards the desk sergeant. Marcus made his way towards the doors, keys already appearing in his hand.

It would be a long, grim drive.

Another body. The killer wasn't ready to stop. And the more she thought about it, the more confident she was that the failed professor in the interrogation room was not their suspect.

CHAPTER TWENTY

Dakota followed Marcus through the sliding glass doors of the library. She frowned as they approached the back of the first level, moving under the crime scene tape lifted by an officer. Marcus lowered his badge, and moved around the set of bookshelves, coming to a stop, facing a small study room in the back.

Agent Marsters was speaking to an older woman with silver hair adorned by a sparkling blue butterfly clip. Marsters paused, holding up a finger, and motioning for Dakota and Marcus to join him.

Dakota's eyes slipped towards the room beyond. She spotted two men in white coats moving about inside. They wore painter's masks as if for fumes. Dakota also spotted an extended hand, resting against the carpet, motionless.

"They still haven't moved the body," Dakota murmured, and Marcus just nodded.

They reached Marsters, and Dakota said, "What happened?"

The man from Homeland Security glanced at her; he was no longer wearing his large hat. But his features, as before, were haggard. The silver trim along his brow and temples stood out in part because of the sweat.

He shook his head. "She suffocated," he said, frowning towards the door. "That's all the coroner knows for now."

The woman he'd been speaking to, though, cleared her throat, and said, "Actually, the *coroner*," she said, with an insistent tilt of pale eyebrows, "would like to have some more time before they move the body."

Dakota took a moment to catch up, but then she glanced at the woman with the butterfly clip. "You're the coroner?"

The woman gave a single nod.

Marcus extended a hand in greeting, which she refused, by showing her own gloved hand. "Been poking and prodding; better if I don't." She had a slow, but assured way of speaking. She continued with, "Unfortunately, when I was going over the crime scene, I found some things that might be of note. There was no sign of forced entry. No sign of a struggle. And the door was locked."

"From the inside?"

"No," she said. "They removed it with bolt cutters. But there was a bike lock."

Dakota glanced towards Marsters. He said, "We are already checking it for prints. But we're not hopeful."

Dakota nodded and glanced back at the coroner. Figures were now moving out of the small study room, avoiding the agents by stepping between two rows of bookshelves.

Dakota frowned at the room. "When was time of death?"

The coroner shook her head. "That was why I've been poking and prodding. And also why I want more time. I think she might have been killed hours ago. Maybe even last night."

Dakota stiffened. "*Last* night?"

"Maybe not that late. I can't tell yet. I don't even know what gas was used."

Dakota held up a hand. "You're sure a gas was used?"

"Oh, yes. Very sure. Young women don't suffocate sitting in a study room. Something was pumped into the room to cause all the oxygen to deplete. It was slow, so she wouldn't have even known. She would have just been irritable, cranky at first. But eventually, she would've fallen unconscious."

"No windows," Marcus said, nodding through the open door.

Dakota frowned, following her partner's gaze then returned her attention to the coroner. "So how come no one found her if she died hours ago?"

"She might have been missed," Marsters said. "We're talking with the librarians, and the student assistants. So far, no one saw anything. We're looking for a better timeframe."

"Are there cameras?" Dakota said.

"Yes. Though not at every exit. Most of the main entrances, though, under video surveillance."

Dakota frowned. "We need that footage."

"Of course," Marsters replied. "I'll send it over."

"Another school," Marcus murmured beneath his breath.

Dakota was nodding. Another school indeed. Someone was out there targeting people related to universities and colleges. She wasn't sure why. But there were too many coincidences to think otherwise.

She closed her eyes briefly, trying not to glance in the direction of the corpse. Trying to think. "We had a suspect in custody but I'm thinking more and more he's the wrong guy."

"There's another thing," said Marsters. "He left a note this time."

Dakota and Marcus looked over sharply. The Homeland Security agent pulled his phone from his pocket, turning it towards her to show a picture on the screen. "You can check the crime scene yourself, once they're out if you want. There isn't much. But here's what he left."

Dakota frowned at the image, glancing through the door of the study room to see if she could make it out for herself.

Marcus was also scowling.

Someone had pushed a small note card beneath the door, which simply read. *Two more by tonight.*

"Is that it?" Dakota said quickly. "Was there anything on the back?"

"Nothing. It's with the lab. They're running prints, making sure it's safe to handle."

Dakota pressed her teeth tightly together. "Two more tonight," she muttered to Marcus. "That's going to be difficult for him if it was Burke."

"You still think it might be him?"

She didn't say anything, but grimly gave a small, quick shake of her head.

Her eyes darted around the space. It was a corner room, concealed by the bookshelves. Whoever had come through had known the place. They must've researched it before. Which meant they would have known the cameras. She wouldn't have been surprised if they had avoided being caught on them but at least that was somewhere they could start.

She shifted uncomfortably, glancing towards the body just visible past the open door.

Another woman, college-aged. Another completely different school. The targets seemed arbitrary. The connection was somehow tied to their academic careers. But why?

What was the killer after?

What did he want?

Dakota took a couple of steps forward now, moving past the coroner and Agent Marsters. She frowned through the open door, her eyes darting along the room.

She glanced towards a textbook open on the table, then a laptop bag left draped over one chair. On the floor, she spotted a discarded backpack, the zipper open wide like the mouth of some toad, the zippers dangling like dewdrops, upside down.

She sighed, glancing towards the body now.

The woman had fallen from the chair, hitting the floor, one arm extending towards the door like an arrow.

She glanced back towards the table.

Her eyes narrowed. "What sort of book is that?" she said slowly.

"Excuse me?" Marsters asked from behind her.

But Dakota stepped forward again, peering through the room, past a man in a white coat who was taking samples from the victim with cotton swabs.

Her eyes were on the textbook. Open to page 143.

She tapped the man on the shoulder. "Could you close the book, please?"

The forensics guy looked up, looked past her, and glanced to Marsters.

The twitching agent nodded once.

The book closed, and Dakota read the cover.

"*Chemistry 101,*" she murmured. She felt a flicker of... Of *something.*

Chemistry 101... that mattered, didn't it? If the killer had scoped out the library before attacking, what if he'd also known student schedules? What if he'd also been looking for a particular *person.* Not just an opportunity...

"What is it, Agent Steele?" Marsters called after her.

She could feel their eyes on her, watching closely.

She paused, biting her lip, then looked back. She gave a single shrug. "I think... I think this might be more personal than we're giving it credit for."

"How so?" Marcus asked.

Dakota glanced back at the textbook, frowning.

How so, indeed.

That was the question of the hour, wasn't it?

CHAPTER TWENTY ONE

"Such morons!" he exclaimed, laughing and glancing into the rearview mirror as he moved hastily along the highway, in the opposite direction of his last project. Two police cars were speeding *away* from him. He felt a rush of exhilaration, pounding his fist against the dashboard. "Idiots!" he screamed, spittle flecking the mirror. "Hah!" he crowed, pumping a fist.

He reached down to turn up the music. Opera swelled inside the cramped, sweltering cabin of his old sedan.

He kept to the speed limit, following a truck loaded with lumber. His eyes darted along the lumber, trying to gauge by the evidence what the man's project was. Two by fours, a couple of longer planks. Some nice trim wedged between two of the boards...

In his mind he pictured all the things he might be able to do with the very same assortment.

He liked piecing things together.

One of his favorite hobbies was woodwork.

Of course, it had never been his favorite hobby the same way that playing with chemicals had been.

He smiled as he merged slowly, hitting his blinker, and allowing another motorist to pass. The other driver blared his horn.

But the chemist was in too good a mood to allow some grumpy-guss to spoil his excitement. He was humming now, along with the music, waving one finger in the air beneath his nose like a conductor's wand.

The sheep couldn't be blamed for bleating, could they?

The cops were no different of course.

"Stupid, stupid—stoooopiiid!" he sang along with the opera, using his own lyrics. He cackled as he turned off the highway.

It had taken them so long to find her, too. It had only taken *him* a few minutes to locate the particular target he'd wanted. He'd checked the library out for nearly a week before noticing Sanna's schedule.

He hadn't known her name at the time. But three days ago, he'd introduced himself. Sanna. Chem 101. He nodded. And she always chose one of three study rooms. He was glad she'd ended up in the back, corner room on that particular day.

He would have hated to change plans.

But even for that he had a contingency. He always came with alternative routes.

That was the best way to strategize, wasn't it?

"Stupid, stupid—morons," he murmured to himself.

This was the problem with the country, after all. He was surrounded by such idiots. How couldn't they see?

Well... now he was making them see.

He grinned, leering in the rearview mirror, and moving hastily up the highway, following the GPS device as it cheerfully barked out instructions barely audible over the crooning of the falsetto voice on his radio.

In the back of the car he had a pile of books he'd stolen from the library. He'd hidden them in his bag after tearing off the barcodes to avoid triggering the security system.

The cameras above the door, of course, had been down for maintenance. Every fifteen days, they would reboot the system for one hour.

He wasn't supposed to know that.

But there were a lot of things he wasn't supposed to know.

Others simply wouldn't pay attention.

And so he'd been clear... concise.

Two more by tonight...

How much more obvious could he get?

If they weren't able to solve it this time...

Well that was their own damn fault, wasn't it?

He'd given them every opportunity possible.

He was humming now along with the music, reaching into the passenger seat and lifting the second cooler he'd brought with him.

This one...

Now *this one* was special.

He stroked the metal lid, humming as he did like someone taking care of a pet.

Pets were stupid, though. Bags of poop and yearning... He couldn't fathom why other apes cottoned on to the fuzzy, whiskery critters.

For that's what he was... All he was.

Some cousin to some ape evolved over millions of years...

But *time* didn't instill *value*. People thought they were so special. But all one had to do was look out a window. Traffic flowed past, quicker, faster. Thousands of people moving about their day. Thousands more in thousands of cities... Millions... Billions... hundreds of billions over the course of human history. And all of them consigned to this single, small dust speck...

He snorted.

To think someone was *so* important... *so* valuable?

No... no more valuable than a grain of sand. And why did it matter to toss sand? To step on a bug? To tear a leaf off a plant?

What he was doing was no different than pruning.

Just because the others didn't see it that way, why should it matter?

In fact, why should he care at all what evolved apes thought of him?

He let out a shuddering little breath of excitement...

He knew he was right. And they were all so dumb.

Yes... yes he would do it tonight.

Two more...

One of them... he swallowed, feeling a jolt of nerves. But he scowled deeply at this, his own mind lashing him with accusation.

No second-guessing. No hesitation. He refused to allow it.

Even this was just chemical reaction. Besides... did he even have a choice? It wasn't like finite beings in a closed system could create options, was it? No... everything was pre-determined. The chemicals in his brain, the firing of the synapses wouldn't help anyone.

Certainly not with what came next.

Two more by tonight.

One of them... himself.

It had to be. That was what he'd planned from the very beginning. He wasn't about to wuss out over some flare of fear. What would that make him?

Nothing more than an ape?

He wasn't anyway...

He shook his head at this thought, sneering.

No... he was going to die tonight. He'd already decided on it.

But the second victim?

Now that one was special. His hand still trailed against the lid of his closed lunchbox. His knuckles rapped against the metal.

He smiled again. A very special concoction for a very special night.

His last night on Earth.

Her last night, also.

This project, more than any, was the one he'd been looking forward to the most.

CHAPTER TWENTY TWO

Dakota paced the small bike path outside the college library, frowning as she did. Marcus was still speaking with Marsters. The coroner was finishing up. But Dakota had needed some time to think. To piece it all together...

Her phone was in her hand, and she was spinning it now. Agent Bonet had contacted her again... Another small text with a friendly smile. *Hope you're doing okay! Loved the most recent work newsletter—did you see the sloth?*

She frowned at the message, still twisting her phone. She *had* seen the sloth. Had read the newsletter. But she couldn't tell if Bonet was being serious or not. What had he loved about it?

It hadn't even registered as interesting to Dakota. Unless... was he making fun of the way one of their coworkers had replied with a video of her cats?

Dakota shook her head. She knew she was overthinking it. But she did *not* enjoy teasing coworkers. It was something she had a particular aversion towards. Gossip was something that, by force of personality alone, she often curtailed in her circles.

Thankfully, Agent Clement was *not* the type to gossip. From Marcus, a comment about loving something was never a veiled attempt to mock it. A sort of pinpointing, finger-jutting, attention-directing ploy.

If Marcus said he loved something... he meant it. But Bonet's message didn't make sense... *Did you see the sloth?* She shook her head, muttering as she did.

She was overthinking. She knew she was.

She let out a faint breath, forcing herself to refocus on the case. She walked beneath a tangle of tree branches, stepping quickly to the side as a cyclist whirred past, calling out. "Sorry!"

She narrowly avoided being bludgeoned by a shouldered bookbag.

She frowned, having stepped off the road into mulch. Carefully, she stomped her foot, dislodging the brown strands of bark, and glared after the cyclist. Adjusting her suit, she moved back to the path, moving off the red bricks onto the gray cobble up the middle of the path. The heat was oppressive, and she instantly found herself wanting a drink. Still, she swallowed and pressed on.

Ahead, in the center of a small, marble fountain, a geyser of water shot into the air, splashing down the basin, into the bowl.

Dakota tapped her fingers against her thigh, still thinking, and then... almost by instinct, she lifted her phone again. *What do you mean?* She said, typing and sending it quickly to Bonet.

She felt a flash of relief as she sent it. Better to ask than assume, wasn't it?

That's what Coach Little often said. Ask, don't assume... he called it *making meaning.*

She bit her lip, considering this... And then, she scrolled to her contacts, moved towards the most recent calls and dialed... She raised the phone, reaching the marble fountain now, and staring at the spray as her device attempted to connect.

He answered on the third ring.

"Tastee?" said the rasping, familiar voice of her old coach.

The moment she heard his voice, she felt a flush of relief, as if she'd walked into a heated home from cold weather.

Dakota felt a lump form in her throat out of nowhere, and she paused, standing on the path beneath an overarching tree. She inhaled shakily, her feet shuffling on red and gray cobblestone. She swallowed. "Coach?" she murmured.

She felt another flare of emotion. Over the last month, since she'd stopped drinking, she'd occasionally felt *strange.* As if not quite sure where a sudden onset of feeling was originating. Now, though, as she stood there, she held back a shaking breath.

She shook her head, certain her poor night's sleep from before was contributing to this strange reaction.

"You good, Tastee?" her coach said. "Shit, you ain't drinkin' again are ya?"

"No, no, it's not..." She trailed off, shaking her head, though there was no way the coach could see. She was accustomed to Little's blunt confrontation style. Accustomed to the way he often went straight to the heart of an issue, indifferent if he bruised a rib along the way.

She loved this about him.

"I..." She wasn't sure why she'd called. Perhaps just to hear a familiar voice. Perhaps as a way to offset the sour taste left in her mouth after talking with her old man. Little had been the father-figure she'd never had. A cussing, fighting, hard-nosed, stiff-necked man who'd often let her live on his couch during the rough years.

He'd personally taken her under his wing, training her in his gym.

Dakota swallowed back a lump and said, "Hey." It wasn't exactly a

104

heartwarming greeting. She wasn't sure what else to say, though. Marcus was the one who liked words. And now, she felt at a distinct lack.

"Hey yourself," Little replied. He paused a moment, and she could see in her mind's eye his wizened brow bunching up over his white eyebrows. He would be nibbling on the corner of his lip, like she so often remembered him doing. After a second, he said, "What's the matter?"

For a moment, she considered denying it. But then again, she had called for a reason. A small part of her didn't want to admit that the phone call with her father was prompting this new call. Sometimes she wondered what it would have been like to have Coach Little as a father. He wasn't. And never could be. That role was reserved for her old man. Now, decades later, she was beginning to regret all the missed birthdays, conversations, connection.

"I'm working a case."

"What type of case?"

"A guy killing women with chemicals."

"Christ. It used to be enough to use your fists. What's this world coming to?"

"He's escalating. He left a note at the last crime scene. He's been killing someone every day. But he's going to kill two more." This, she knew, was a tad over the line... The FBI wouldn't smile on her revealing classified information via phone... but in her mind, Little was as reliable as they came.

"Dammit. That's rough stuff, Dakota." She knew it was serious given how he didn't use her nickname.

She said, "I don't know why I'm calling, if I'm honest."

"No need for an excuse to call. Sometimes support is the missing piece."

She wasn't exactly sure what this meant. "Yeah. Yeah, that makes sense."

"How's your partner handling?"

"Great. Like always."

"Glad to know you have someone who's going to watch your back."

"Yeah. Me too. I'm just," she trailed off again. She didn't know what to ask. What to say. Didn't know what she was forgetting. Part of her wanted to turn and march right back up the cobblestone path. She could still see figures moving in and out of the library. Another part of her wanted to sit beneath the tree, tuck her legs under her, and cry.

She wasn't sure where these emotions were coming from. The lack of drink, the talk with her father, the coach's familiar voice; it was all playing a role.

"Well," she said slowly. "This guy is a bit of a loner. He likes isolating his victims."

"He familiar with them?"

"Still determining that."

"Alright. Because, don't forget, some of the tougher opponents you faced at the gym were your training partners."

"How could I forget that?" she said, ruefully, rubbing at her chin. "You would make us fight every weekend. Without the pads."

"Damn right I did. Familiarity breeds contempt, they say. But it also trains you to outlast your opponent. You can't pull tricks against someone who knows them all."

Dakota snorted, remembering more than one occasion when she had been stuck in a boxing ring during training camp with someone who had worked in Coach Little's gym. He seemed to take a particular delight in pitting her against people who knew her style.

Now, though, her brow flickered into a frown. Her coach was right. People who were familiar with their victims made deadlier killers. They knew how to anticipate the threat.

But also... she remembered a particular opponent at the gym.

"Do you remember Randy?"

"*Bones* Randy?"

"I think so. It would've been a while ago."

"I don't forget a fighter who trained here."

Dakota clicked her tongue. "Right well, Bones was one of *those* training partners. But you kicked him out of the gym."

"I remember that too," came Little's voice. There was a pause, and in the background, Dakota heard the sound of skipping ropes, and gloves hitting heavy bags. Like always, her old mentor was at the gym.

"Yeah," she said, slowly, "but as I was thinking, I'm wondering if maybe familiarity can turn dangerous."

"If I remember correctly, Randy was the one who made things dangerous. He started trying to deal in my gym. You know how I feel about that."

Dakota could tell her coach was starting to get angry. Sometimes, his temper could flare up with very little notice. She leaned against the rough truck of the nearest tree and said quickly, "I'm not accusing you of doing anything wrong. You made the right call. But didn't Bones try to sue you?"

"He failed."

Dakota nodded to herself, tucking her tongue inside her cheek, frowning in thought.

"Think you'll be by anytime soon?"

"I don't know. I was talking to my dad recently. I might stop by to visit, and pick something up."

"Hell. That's changed. What happened?"

"You know, maybe we can talk about that later. Sorry, I probably should go."

In part, she had spotted Marcus appearing on the steps outside the library. But also, she simply didn't want to rehash the issues she had with her father.

Casper was capable of taking a hint. Though usually, he would barrel right through it. This time, though, instead of pressing her on the issue, he started shouting something, his words muffled as if he had lowered his phone. "Use the right," he yelled. "Your other right, idiot. He's going to knock your head off."

"Coach?" Dakota said, louder. "Hey, I'm heading out. It's been a blast."

"All right, Tastee. Happy to talk. Any time. I mean it."

"Of course. Thanks."

But he cleared his throat and said, more insistently. "Dakota, I really do mean it. If you need anything, don't hesitate to call."

She felt that same lump in her throat. But as she bid farewell, her mind was spinning. She lowered the phone, and began moving back down the cobblestone path. The particular opponent she'd been thinking of had been kicked out of the gym. He'd been a danger to the other fighters. There was nothing like rejection that could spur someone mentally unstable to violence. But the issue, as she considered it, wasn't just romantic rejection. Too many women at different schools. No, something else was at play.

What if the killer wasn't just a chemistry student, but a student who'd faced disciplinary action or academic failure? It would fit the profile. It would give a motive behind the personal nature of the crimes. The connection between them. But which school? Was she just picking at straws?

She frowned, trying to think through her options. And if it was because of an expulsion, or something similar, perhaps his anger wasn't directed solely at *one* school, but the whole system. He'd targeted women from multiple schools, after all... was it simply lashing out? A deep hatred?

She sighed, trying to consider the options.

Marcus had spotted her, and was now raising a hand, his expression solemn.

She picked up her pace, moving hastily back across the ground, towards Agent Clement.

The killer was going to strike again. This time targeting two people. There was no time to think too long about it. No time to squander; she picked up her pace, nodding to herself.

If the killer was rejected, it was possibly romantic. She couldn't rule it out. But also, the academic nature of the victims suggested they should look at schools as well. Disciplinary hearings. Suspensions. Expulsions. There were a lot of schools in the area. A lot of chemistry departments. It would take some time to parse it all out.

But two more lives were on the line. Dakota had to do something.

CHAPTER TWENTY THREE

Dakota sat in the small, sweltering office space they had been allowed to borrow from the local police department. Marcus was playing with a desk toy, tapping a finger against a floating metal flowerpot, upheld by electromagnetic force. He was smiling as he poked at the pot, and every so often, he let out a sigh and returned his attention to the computer screen.

Dakota didn't blame him. Marcus had the task of contacting the victims' families, and asking them to send a comprehensive list of their romantic history. The emails were slowly coming in, now that Marcus had finished the phone calls, and he was waiting to compile a list to cross reference them.

"Did you make sure to ask for physical descriptions?" She said. "Remember, he might be using an alias."

But Marcus nodded. "Already done," he said. "Nothing so far. Our most recent victim was too young to have much of a dating history. Only one boyfriend. And they were still together."

Dakota felt a flash of anxiety as she shook her head in frustration, and returned to her own compilation.

Another email showed up in her inbox. She opened it, and downloaded the spreadsheet

"Are the schools complying with the directive?" Marcus asked.

Dakota nodded. "The most recent murder seems to have done it. I'm not getting any red tape." She scanned the new list of information, funneling it to one of the tech agents back in Virginia who was helping to compile a new database with all the students in a fifty mile radius who had been suspended or expelled. She had especially requested to highlight chemistry majors.

Now, the two of them were waiting for their email lists to populate.

Time was ticking. And both of them, despite whatever distractions they managed to conjure with the desk ornament, were all too aware of the killer's threat.

Two more victims by tonight.

Dakota wished she had gotten better sleep the night before.

But now, as she tapped her fingers against the desk, she couldn't help but hold back the rising sense of anxiety and fear.

One way or another, she knew eventually, she would have to catch this man before he killed again.

"All right," she said suddenly, tapping the screen. "That's the last school."

"I have the dating history in. I'm not seeing anything, Dakota. Even with the physical descriptions. None of the names match. None of the cars they drive match. And their descriptions don't match."

Dakota hesitated, but then nodded once. "All right, call it a wash. Come help me with this."

Dakota began sending the files over to her partner as well.

He looked at her across the desk, shaking his head. "What makes you so sure that this guy was rejected somehow?"

Dakota said, "It fits the MO. There's something personal about these crimes. But it's still one step removed. Like there's some personal stake in it for the killer but the victims aren't the important part."

"So you think this was a chemistry student who was expelled?"

"Or ridiculed. The boyfriend option was still on the table. But if you're sure there's no connections..."

Marcus shook his head. "All I'm saying this might be a big list."

Dakota nodded. "I don't have any better ideas, Marcus." She had returned her attention to the computer screen, her eyes narrowed, her teeth set tightly together. "And, I'm not about to allow him to get away with it."

Without further protest, Marcus also began sorting through the email chain she had sent him.

Dakota watched in real time as one of the tech agents back in Quantico messaged her that the database had been updated. She followed the link the guy had sent, and opened the new search engine.

It would be temporary, but would allow her to search through any student who had been suspended or expelled for whatever reason.

"All right," she said, slowly. "I think the list is too broad. This one isn't even within a hundred miles of here. Let me see if I can get him to change that." She trailed off, glancing at the top of the webpage. But then she nodded quickly. Tapping a finger against the screen. "No, up there, at the top, you can slide the bar."

Marcus grunted. By the looks of things, he was already deep in research.

Dakota went quiet as well, frowning, slowly peeling back the layers of information.

She limited the graduation range. Keeping it within the last ten years. She limited by major. Only the sciences. Then, with a frown, she went further and kept it solely to chemistry majors.

As she did, the list grew narrower.

She tapped a finger against her lips as she studied the information.

"It shows the disciplinary reasons in the far column," Marcus said with a murmur.

"Right. Remove anything that has to do with academic performance," Dakota shot back.

She spotted on their shared page as changes were made in real time. Marcus began tweaking some of the names as well.

Dakota typed quickly in the messenger box to their support, "I'm removing any disciplinary action that ended in reinstatement at the school. If they came back, cut it."

She got a thumbs up in response. Now, the list was looking much smaller.

Once Marcus cleared out the academic disciplinary cases, Dakota frowned.

In a fifty mile radius, from only chemistry majors in the last decade who were suspended or expelled without ever returning to complete an academic career, who still lived in the area, there were only ten viable suspects.

But of those ten, as she clicked through their information, only eight of them were still alive.

One had been found dead in his apartment five years ago. Another had died in a car crash.

She scrolled on. Of the eight remaining names, she began reading the reasons for the disciplinary action.

Whenever she came to a keyword that involved drinking, or profanity she also removed this. Some of the suspensions had only been for a week, or a few days. The students themselves had removed the applications.

Most of them now had jobs. Most of them, by the looks of things, were doing fine.

But there was one in particular that caught her eye.

"Look at this one," she said quickly. "Fourth from the top."

Marcus leaned in, frowning at the page.

Dakota waited, allowing him to read the disciplinary reason for the expulsion of Tommy Barrett.

"He brought a gun to class?" Marcus said, scowling.

"No. Look closer. A water gun. But it was filled with a type of acid."

Marcus scowled. "Why wasn't there any disciplinary action?"

"Looks like he didn't actually end up using it."

"Where is this guy now? Unemployed?"

"Looks like it. But I have a home address. He still lives with his father."

Dakota clicked on the link for Tommy Barrett. The young man's profile picture appeared. There was no DMV photo, as by the looks of things he didn't have a license.

She frowned, staring at the picture. The figure in question was heavy, with a bowl cut, and blonde, streaked hair. He had sunken eyes, and bulging cheeks. He looked exhausted in the photo on his social media profile.

"All right, look here, he posted something three weeks ago."

Marcus lowered the lid of his laptop, and, frowning, circled the desk to peer over her shoulder. The two of them both read the article that Tommy Barrett had posted. It was a strange article, from a fringe political site, discussing the Uni-Bomber.

"He goes dark online after posting this. The murders started only a week after," Marcus murmured.

Dakota was already pushing to her feet. "I think we should pay Mr. Barrett a visit."

CHAPTER TWENTY FOUR

Marcus pulled their loaner to a halt outside the small, ranch-style single-story. Dakota had spotted more than one swimming pool in backyards—a staple of the Arizona suburbs. Now, as she exited the vehicle, double-checking her phone to make sure they'd arrived at the correct location, her eyes were fixated on the figure standing at the back of the home, with a long pool cleaner in hand.

The man swiped the cleaner through the water and lifted a bunch of old, dead leaves, ladling them onto the side of the pool.

The faint scent of chlorine tinged the hot air. Dakota carefully avoided ants crawling along the ground—she'd heard Marcus yelp on more than one occasion at the last crime scene where the small fire ants had nipped her partner.

She missed Virginia. Missed her orchids and reasonable temperatures.

Even now, having exited the heavily air-conditioned vehicle to step out beneath the blistering sun, she could feel a thin glaze of sweat forming across her forehead.

She waved as she walked up the driveway, raising her badge in the same hand. "Hello!" she called. "Mr. Barrett?"

The man paused, tilting at his forehead with the back of his hand, adjusting his baseball cap. He sighed, and shot a glance back over the iron fence. He watched the two agents approach him up his driveway, his eyes darting between them.

"Hello," he said slowly.

Dakota studied the man's face. He looked similar to the images she'd found on social media for their suspect, but Tommy Barrett didn't have facial hair, and his features were about twenty years younger.

This, she decided, was the owner of the residence.

"FBI," Dakota said conversationally. She tried to keep her tone neutral. No sense in alarming the man. Often this only set up obstacles. She said, "Is your son home?"

The figure turned fully now, still gripping the pool cleaner in one hand. It dangled behind him, into the pool like some metal umbilical cord.

He frowned at Dakota. "FBI? What's he done?"

Marcus was joining them now. He came to a halt just a step past Dakota, gesturing with one hand vaguely over his shoulder, as if accepting a baton, but also indicating their car. "Nothing we know yet," Marcus said with a polite dip of his head. "Just wanted to speak with him. Is he here?"

The older Barrett scowled though. He dropped the pool cleaner. The metal and plastic handle *clacked* against the side of the pool. The blue water served as a backdrop as he marched towards the agents, his frown creasing his features deeply.

"Don't try that double-talk with me," he said firmly. "The Good Lord knows my boy ain't perfect. What's the dang kid done this time?"

Marcus hesitated. Dakota didn't speak, allowing the big man to fill in the blanks. For her part, she was studying Mr. Barrett, analyzing his posture, the sag in his shoulders. He'd dropped the pool cleaner, leaving the task unfinished behind him. His hands were both clenched, but it seemed more defensive than anything.

He also spoke with a slight quaver to his voice. A trembling in his tone that came from pain. His eyes were almost pleading as they darted between Dakota and Marcus. "Something I can pay for? Or something I need a lawyer for?"

Marcus shook his head. Dakota said, "We just need to speak with him. Is he here?"

"No ma'am," he said, shaking his head and removing his baseball cap to fan at his face. "He ain't. Wish he were. Haven't seen him in a couple days now," Barrett sighed.

Dakota studied the man further. She had always prided herself on reading nonverbal cues. As far as she could tell, the suspect's father was telling the truth. Then again, often, sociopathy was hereditary.

So she said, "Mind if we take a look around inside the house?"

He looked directly into her eyes. He nodded once. "I do mind."

Marcus shifted uncomfortably. He said, "Sir... Do you have any idea *where* your boy might be?"

The man hesitated. He began to shake his head, but then paused, biting his lip. He sighed, and murmured. "I won't lie. Not even on behalf of Tommy. He's... probably with those deadbeat friends of his. They spend time by the old sawmill. Place is a trash hole."

Dakota was moving now, along the house, out of the line of sight from Mr. Barrett. She heard him clear his throat, followed by the sound of a creaking gate. "Hey!" he called out after her. "Hey, you need a warrant!"

But Dakota peered into the garage window. Only a single, old beaten-up truck. The man's son didn't own a car. Or at least, didn't have a driver's license and so *wasn't supposed to* own a car.

She frowned, moving along the side of the house, and peering through windows. The gate closed with a *clang* behind her.

She heard the stamp of footsteps, and glanced back, frowning, to see Mr. Barrett walk hastily alongside Marcus, frowning as Dakota approached the front door.

"I said you're not welcome!" he snapped. "This is private property."

"What are you hiding, sir?" Dakota asked, turning sharply.

He looked her dead in the eyes. "Nothing," he said. "As the Lord is my witness. But you still haven't told me what Tommy is supposed to have—"

"We're investigating him for the murders of three women," Dakota said firmly.

Mr. Barrett went still, eyes the size of saucers. A hand darted to his lips, and he swallowed, his Adam's apple bobbing.

Dakota watched him, then her eyes narrowed. "I can't help but notice," she said slowly, "That you aren't denying it."

"W-what?" he said, dazedly. "No... no... I don't think..." he trailed off, shaking his head. His hand, still near his lips, was also trembling horribly. Dakota studied him, her brow etched in deep creases. She shot a look towards Marcus, and he shrugged back at her.

She pointed towards the man's house. "May we see inside? We don't mean to intrude, sir. But we need to speak with your son."

The older man let out a shaking breath, but then, as if in a trance, he reached slowly towards his pocket. Dakota tensed, but then he withdrew a set of keys, with equally slow motions. With dejected steps, he walked up the stairs towards the small house. He was shaking his head, murmuring as he did.

He pushed through the house, gesturing over his shoulder for the agents to follow.

Dakota was surprised by this. She'd thought that he was intentionally holding back in order to protect his son.

But now, at the mention of the charges, it was as if the wind had been taken from his sails. He pushed the door open and waved down a hall. "His room is on the right. He hasn't been home, like I said, in two days..." he trailed off, his face pale. "Careful..." he said, swallowing, "careful for the glass containers. He told me some of them were corrosive."

Dakota and Marcus moved slowly into the dingy, small house. Their hands were on their unbuttoned holsters, and they moved slowly down the hall. Dakota's eyes darted along a sofa, towards a small television, into a kitchen with no dishwasher and an old microwave. Marcus glanced through the window in the back of the kitchen, towards the pool. No movement in the backyard. No shed. The garage had been empty when Dakota had checked.

The two of them, then, shoulder to shoulder, moved down the hall, towards the indicated bedroom. Both of them breathed in faint, shallow puffs of air, their eyes wide as they moved. Dakota followed slowly along, also tense.

"Mr. Barrett," Dakota said suddenly, "Please, if you don't mind, step outside." She didn't want an unknown quantity lurking behind them.

The man was barely coherent, though. He took a single step back onto the concrete porch, and just gaped after them through the open door.

The air-conditioned house was still quite warm, and the sweat prickling Dakota's forehead now trickled down her temple.

She moved along the doors, glancing in the various rooms. The bathroom was small, empty. No basement by the look of things. The next room a pantry—also empty save some boxes of cereal and some strange cleaning solutions with odd markings on them.

"What are these?" Dakota called over her shoulder.

"Ummm... Supplies. Tommy... Tommy likes making things," Barrett called back, swallowing as he spoke.

Dakota and Marcus pushed open one door. A bedroom. The bedframe was against the ground. The closet too small to hide in. They moved on to the next room.

"That's his!" the voice called from behind them. "Just... be careful! Don't knock anything off his shelf.

Dakota and Marcus both pulled their weapons now, moving slowly, tense. Marcus tried the door and the handle clicked as it slowly turned.

Dakota pushed against the frame with her shoulder, both of them breathing in silent, huffing gasps. Neither of them backing down. She shot a final look towards the door, but their suspect's father was motionless, dumbfounded, and frozen in place.

The door opened, and she went still.

Marcus peered over her. The two of them found themselves facing a very *odd* room.

There were a couple of water guns resting against the back wall. A metal shelf covered in glass containers, beakers, and colorful test tubes were arranged near a half-open window. The air-conditioning unit in the room was turned off, and the space was even warmer than outside. The space smelled faintly of sweat and salt. Dakota eyed the beakers and jars along the wall. All of them containing strangely hued or textured liquids or emulsions. The labels were printed clearly with letters and numbers like *A2*. Or *B13*. But she wasn't able to identify any of them.

She shot a look towards Marcus and shrugged once.

He nodded back at her, glancing towards the bed in the back of the room. Someone had turned it on its side, the blankets wedged against the wall, the wooden frame having been repurposed, nailed together to create a workbench. On the bench there were burn marks and strange, corrosive stains.

Dakota glanced at a couple of the posters on the wall. One was an elemental chart of geek culture. Replacing elements with magic spells from role-playing games or video games. Another was a picture of an old man with a flat forehead and wide, blinking eyes. She didn't recognize the portrait, but Marcus murmured, "Oppenheimer."

"Who?"

Marcus was slowly holstering his weapon. "A scientist," Marcus muttered. "He created the atomic bomb.

Dakota scowled at the words. Marcus said, "He once called himself *death, the destroyer of worlds.*"

Dakota let out a faint huff of air, turning once again, once she'd scanned the room, to face the open door. A figure appeared there, and she startled. But it was only their suspect's father. He had a tear trailing along his cheek. "Did Tommy really kill someone?" he whispered, sniffing as he did. "I... I never should have sent him off to school. He wasn't ready..."

Dakota holstered her weapon as well. "This sawmill," she said, "Where he spends time with his friends... where is it?"

But Mr. Barrett was shaking his head now. "Tommy..." he swallowed, wiping angrily at his cheek. "Tommy wouldn't go there if he... if he did something like this."

"So where might he go?" Marcus said.

The father hesitated, frowning. Dakota wondered what it might feel like to have an old man who actually cared.

The man was shaking his head, though, rubbing at his eyes and emitting a long sigh. "He could be anywhere. He takes taxis. Or gets rides from his friends."

Dakota glanced around the room. She said, slowly, "Your son was expelled two years ago."

He nodded. "And if I had known Tommy would turn violent, I would have said something myself. I didn't know. I believed him about the water guns."

Marcus looked troubled as the man spoke. Dakota, though, glanced past the rows of beakers and test tubes, her eyes peering out the window into the side yard. She could just glimpse the top of the metal gate that led to the swimming pool.

"How did he take it—the expulsion?" she said, slowly. She glanced back towards Mr. Barrett.

"Not well," he said slowly. The man looked like he was torn. Clearly, he cared for his son. But up to this point, Dakota was given the impression he was also an honest man. Now, he seemed trapped. The look of pain across his face was all too apparent. He said, though, "It wasn't like he was homicidal," he said suddenly, frowning. "He just really wanted to go to school. He'd been dreaming about it since he was a child. He had big aspirations. Getting expelled really took it out of him."

Dakota shook her head. "According to the report we saw, he took a water gun loaded with an acidic solution to class. He threatened to spray people with it. It sounded like he was causing a disturbance, and he felt as if one of his teachers was treating him unfairly by giving him a lower grade than he deserved."

Mr. Barrett nodded. "Tommy can sometimes be too confident that he is in the right. He has a strong sense of justice and fairness. Especially if he thinks someone is crossing him."

"Strong enough to take revenge?" Dakota said, firmly. Her hand rested above her belt on her hip

Tommy's father ran a hand over his pale, weary face. He gave another small shake. "I don't know," he murmured.

Dakota turned back to glance at the room. Her eyes moved across the desk, with an outlet over the surface. No plugs, no power cords. The desk, though, had a rectangular mark in the dust. A laptop. He must have taken it with him.

"Do you have his number?" Marcus said delicately.

"He doesn't use the phone," said Mr. Barrett. "When he calls for taxis, he uses my phone, or asks his friends."

"What about his computer?" Dakota said.

"He uses it for games. For research. And sometimes he will try to apply to different schools. But the expulsion shows up on his record."

Dakota suddenly went tense. She frowned, considering these words. "He sends emails? You say he was very interested in going to school?"

"It was a dream of his to be a scientist."

"All right, Marcus, let's go." She didn't wait for further comment form the suspect's father. Farewells were not her strong suit.

Briskly, she turned, and marched back out the door. She shot an uncomfortable glance towards the back of Mr. Barrett's head. She thought of her own father, and wondered if he had ever looked like this when she had been making choices as a teenager.

She wondered if her father knew that she had felt as much pain as he did. If her father knew that his choices had affected her.

She shook her head in frustration, and picked up the pace, moving hastily away.

Marcus followed after her, his lips sealed, his footsteps loud against creaking floorboards.

The two of them reached the concrete steps of the porch, and took the cement stairs down to the walkway.

Dakota glanced back. Mr. Barrett was still in his son's room.

She felt a jolt of sadness. Grief. She forced her mind to flit away from her own experience with her father. She said, quietly, "I want to try to send an email to his student address."

"Excuse me?"

The two of them had come to stop by the hood of their car.

Dakota glanced across the glossy surface, reflecting the sunlight. "I want to send an email, and see if we can locate his IP address."

"His student email?"

"Exactly. If school mattered as much to him as his father says, and if he's still applying to schools, there's a chance he still has access to it."

"Did you believe that part about not owning a phone?"

Dakota nodded once. "Also checked before coming. No driver's license, and no phone line. The dad only has one. This is a strange guy, Marcus."

"Strange doesn't mean guilty."

"I never said it did."

Dakota reached for the door handle, using the hem of her sleeve to offset the heat of the metal.

Marcus pulled his door open as well, and slid into the front seat.

Meanwhile, Dakota withdrew her phone, and was already busy typing. The school would likely provide the email address for an expelled student quickly. They had been compliant so far.

And though the sun was still out, when night came, if they didn't hurry, two more women would lose their lives.

CHAPTER TWENTY FIVE

He stepped away from his parked vehicle, peering up at the two-story house at the end of the cul-de-sac. Grass lawns would have been ambitious near the Arizona deserts. Against a backdrop of dunes, and open, rough terrain with the rare interference of scabby vegetation, he glimpsed the glare and glimmer of glass and metal. He scowled in the direction of the building.

He wet his lips, running his tongue along the rough edges. It was hot, the Arizona sun beating down. His hand grazed the hood of his car, but he quickly jerked it away from the scalding metal.

He double checked that he had locked it and then moved towards the house.

Evening was not far off, but he had to prepare.

Just like with the last project, this one had to be timed perfectly.

He paused on the sidewalk, facing the desert beyond the house. As his eyes trailed over the desolate terrain, again, his gaze landed on the large metal and glass structure in the distance.

He frowned in its direction, feeling memories surface: painful memories.

And pain would be the price.

Two more by tonight. He had meant what he'd said but one of the victims would be himself.

The other?

He thought he spotted her window. She lived alone. Of course she did. A shrew like that. Who would ever want to live with her?

His hands clenched at his sides. He could feel a familiar burbling of hatred rising in his gut. But as he stared at her, eyes narrowed, that same hatred began to spread. Small strands of grass jutted along the edge of the driveway. The grass was barely green and could hardly be described as lush.

Most homes in this area came with swimming pools as a requirement.

This particular house, though, matched its owner's personality.

Some amount of gray paint, an untended yard, and no pool... Plain and simple.

As he moved up the driveway, slowly, hands in his pockets now, head ducked in case she still had that security camera over her door, he frowned. He moved slowly, avoiding the driveway for a brief, hesitant second; he wanted to walk on the asphalt.

But this, like everything else, was just societal conditioning.

He fell for it like all the other primates. But he was smarter than the rest of them. And so he stepped onto the grass. These tawdry rules didn't apply to him; his lip curled into a sneer at the thought. So much of society was structured around control. So many people wanted to control him.

He intentionally stamped a few times along the scraggy grass, towards the window where he had spotted the movement.

He leaned forward; even the glass was warm as his nose brushed against it.

The vapor from his breath didn't fog so much as slick the surface

He wiped at the window with the back of his hand, clearing a smudge.

Where was she?

He couldn't see her.

He thought he saw another flicker of motion, but again, he couldn't be certain.

He began to move along the side of the house, slowly; in the distance, he could hear a dog barking. He had never much liked dogs, and they had never liked him. Especially the ones he had experimented on when he'd been younger. Since then, he had graduated to better experiments.

He moved along the side of the house now. He paused, and through an open window thought he could hear faint humming. A radio was crooning in the background.

He paused, peering through another window. He rose on his tiptoes, his hands scraping against the stucco of the gray walls. He gripped the marble windowsill, his fingers tense against the smooth, dusty surface.

The window was cracked. A faint stream of chill wind from the air conditioning swept out into the afternoon sun, causing prickles to rise along his cheeks.

He tried to push the window open a bit further.

But no luck.

The humming was growing louder now; he could hear faint laughter, and a voice. But only one voice, suggesting she was either speaking to herself, or talking on the phone.

He could wait. There was no harm in waiting. Besides, this wasn't where he was going to do it. Following, speculating, and keeping an eye on his projects was all part of the fun.

He lowered his hand from the windowsill, and pushed away, stalking back along the side of the house. No one saw him—none of the neighbors noticed anything; he was a very forgettable man to some.

They wouldn't forget him much longer, though. Soon everyone would know his name.

CHAPTER TWENTY SIX

Dakota sat in the back of their vehicle, frowning at her phone, tensed all of a sudden.

"What is it?" Marcus asked, leaning in next to her. "Did he reply?"

She quickly read the heading of the bold email at the top of the inbox she'd set up. She stared, and then slapped her hand against the dusty dashboard. "Yes—he did! We got it!"

Marcus was lifting his phone up next to his lips where his hand had sagged over the last hour of waiting. Now, though, his voice was tinged with excitement. He said, "Did you hear that Bonet?"

Dakota shifted uncomfortably.

Agent Mark Bonet had been the techie assigned to help them trace Mr. Barrett's IP. She'd already gone on a couple of dates with Bonet, and had been exchanging texts with him over the last few weeks, but now she felt uncomfortable.

She couldn't quite say why. He'd never replied to her message earlier, though she now felt silly for picking at him over it. Still, the tone in Marcus's voice didn't match her own attitude.

She waited uncomfortably as Bonet said, "Loud and clear, Clement. I'm tracking him now. He's using a public Wi-Fi hotspot. Looks like... Yeah, I see him here. He's at a small, private college right now."

Dakota perked up. "Which one?" she said.

Bonet replied, "Larem-Yount College. It's about twenty minutes from your location."

Dakota frowned, hesitating now. She nibbled the corner of her lip, hesitating. "You're sure? It's him?"

Bonet said, "He logged into the email you provided. Pretty sure. Good call, by the way, Dakota."

Marcus glanced over, nodding. "Yeah—nice one."

Dakota shifted uncomfortably, nodding at the praise but keeping her expression neutral. "Thanks much," she said stiffly.

Bonet said, "Jeez, looking at this guy, give him a couple of love-taps from me, won't you Marcus?"

Clement smiled congenially, laughing faintly, taking it as a joke. Dakota wasn't so sure Bonet meant it to be humorous.

"What do you mean?" she said slowly.

Bonet cleared his voice on the other line. He coughed. "I..." He trailed off, then quickly shifting gears, he said, "I just meant this guy's doing some high level shit..."

Dakota winced. She wished she knew how to better navigate these sorts of conversations. She hadn't meant to make Bonet uncomfortable. Bu the more time she spent with the agent, the more she felt... odd about the way he acted.

Not that she was much better, was she?

She could be cold, callous... blunt...

But that was the point, wasn't it? She didn't want to be around someone who only fanned into flame the worst parts of her personality. She needed someone... kinder than she was...

Or maybe she was overthinking it...

Or maybe you're just projecting your father's coldness onto Bonet...

This last thought made her wince. She could only hope this wasn't the case.

Marcus though, leaned in. "Hey, Bonet," he said. "What do you mean by that?"

"Hmm?"

"High level? What do you mean?"

"Oh," Mark said, his voice coming clear and crisp over the cellular connection. "Just that I minored in chemistry. A lot of this stuff is way over my head. I got a glance of the coroner's report. What came back from the lab was... impressive."

"Impressive how?" Dakota said, trying to subdue her strong sense of guilt in favor of a new line of questioning.

"Oh... ummm... Just..." Bonet seemed flustered, but he quickly recovered. "Just that I didn't know many chemistry majors who could pull of creating these sorts of new, stable compounds... at least, not without killing themselves in the process... You know—he's still connected to that Wi-Fi hub. Nothing reported to campus security yet. I'm sending some locals over as well."

"Thanks Bonet," Agent Clement said. "Appreciate the help! We're on our way now."

Marcus was already putting the car in gear. As he pulled away from the curb, moving hastily up the suburban street, the Arizona sunshine was slowly fading, receding against the horizon and retreating to night.

Dakota's fingers tapped in rhythm against the plastic arm rest, frowning through the window as Marcus picked up space, guiding them hastily in the direction of the small private college.

"Think he's already got his next victim?" Marcus murmured.

Dakota was frowning, hesitant. "I..." Something Agent Bonet said was now bothering her. "Do you think..." she trailed off, frowning. What if she'd made a mistake? What did he mean about the chemistry being too *high-level.* No major would be able to come up with those compounds...

Was she missing something?

"The second victim..." she said slowly. "She was... a grad student, right?"

Marcus shot her a sidelong look. "Yeah? So?"

"Did we... when we went through the list... the disciplinary list... The expulsions. Those were all from undergrad, weren't they?"

Marcus frowned as he picked up the pace, keeping within a few miles of the speed limit for now as he tapped a finger against the window GPS, allowing it to guide them to the private college.

Dakota, though, was now hastily returning to the list they'd compiled. She noted the Excel sheet *did* have information from grad programs, but it hadn't been included in the initial list. There were far, far fewer suspensions or expulsions in the collegiate grad courses.

The GPS was chirping now, and Marcus merged onto the highway.

Dakota, though, was studying the information on grad students closely, frowning as she did. A few of the expulsions had been academic in nature. One, for a private Christian college, had been a suspension for missing too many chapels. She removed female students, temporarily. It didn't quite fit the psych profile...

She was left with three names who still lived locally.

She scanned them one at a time. One of the suspects had been arrested for sexual assault. He was currently in prison. Another had been suspended for calling in a fake bomb threat. According to the attached arrest report, though, they hadn't determined any intent. Apparently he'd been drunk at the time and done it on a dare in front of a room full of frat boys.

The last name, though, caught her attention.

Tyler Moore. A grad-student with an internship at a local pharmaceutical lab... Mr. Moore had been accused of poisoning his teacher.

She stared at this last one. "Marcus..." she murmured.

"Only ten minutes left," he replied.

"No," she said quickly. "Not that. Look... wait—no, actually, keep your eyes on the road. But listen to this. Tyler Moore, a grad-student in his second year was expelled for slipping some type of homemade toxic concoction into his professor's morning coffee."

"Excuse me?" Marcus shot her a look, his nose wrinkling.

She shook her head in disbelief, but said. "That was my reaction, but it looks like the police didn't have enough evidence to arrest him. He... yeah, he slowly slipped something into a professor's coffee. The professor in question says it was revenge over giving Mr. Moore a bad grade for missing class."

Dakota tapped her fingers against the armrest, shaking her head uncomfortably.

Marcus was frowning through the windshield now, his hands tight on the steering wheel. "You having doubts about Mr. Barrett?"

Dakota huffed in frustration, shaking her head. "No, no... Just..." She shook her head. "Bonet's comments... What if we weren't looking at grad students, and..."

Marcus frowned at her again. "Where is Mr. Moore?"

Dakota shook her head. "He has a phone number, so we should be able to track him... Here, I'm calling Mark."

She lifted her phone now, allowing the it to ring. After a few seconds, Agent Bonet answered. "Hey Dakota, everything alright?"

"Umm, yeah, fine Mark. Look, can I get a trace on a number?"

"Live number?"

"I can call it."

"Sure, give me a second. Text me the info if you could."

"Sure—here, one second." Dakota's fingers flew across the screen now, and she heard the satisfied grunt of Mark as he received the information. "Right," he said. "Give it a call, could you? Don't need him to pick up for this trick. But the call will expedite."

Marcus and Dakota went silent as, slowly, she entered the number for Mr. Moore and pressed the small, green phone symbol.

And then they waited, tense. The phone rang a few times without connecting, and then went straight to voicemail. But the robotic message said, *The number you are dialing has a voicemail box that is not set up yet. Please—*

She hung up. "You got it?" she asked.

Agent Bonet was clicking his tongue now, but after a few moments, he said, "Yes... yes, pinged off the nearest tower... Mr. Moore is... about half an hour east of you. Near a suburb bordering the desert..." He paused then added, "Actually, he's only a few miles away from a pharmaceutical lab out in the desert."

Dakota frowned. "Is he moving?"

"Looks like he's in a car," replied Bonet. "Here, I'm sending you the address."

Dakota felt her phone buzz, and quickly looked down, clicking the link. She followed it to a map and glanced up at the GPS. "Thanks Mark!" she called out. Then, as she hung up, she said, "Shit."

"What?" Marcus shot back.

"Opposite direction... he's an hour from that college."

Marcus was slowing now, glancing at Dakota. "So what's the call? We can send locals to meet up with one of them."

Dakota hesitated, then shook her head. "No... no we can send cops to meet at both spots, but one of us needs to be there. I'm not trusting boots on the ground with this guy. If he's killed with chemicals, he's prepared to do it again."

"Doesn't mean you have to put yourself in harm's way," Marcus said firmly.

"No, but it's my job to try and stop him. Here... yeah... yeah quick, pull over! I'm going to ping highway patrol. They usually have someone every five miles or so."

Marcus didn't comply right away. He was shaking his head, lips pursed. "Are you sure? What if—"

"No time, Clement!" she snapped. "Please, pull over."

Marcus didn't retort, but instead let out a long sigh, pulling slowly onto the side of the road.

She added a quick, mumbled, "Sorry. Just... here, you head to the college, find Mr. Barrett and bring him in for questioning. I'll go speak with Tyler Moore."

Before Marcus could protest, Dakota flung open the door, and spilled out onto the shoulder, stumbling towards the metal divider and hastily raising her phone, already having speed-dialed the highway patrol.

"Come on," she murmured beneath her breath.

Clement was still frowning at her through his open window, his hazards flashing and illuminating the asphalt. The sun was dipping even lower in the sky.

"Go on!" she called, waving at her partner. "You need to be there, Clement. I trust you."

He huffed in frustration, but then nodded once. With a final glance of concern through his window, he merged back onto the highway and began picking up speed again, his hazards still blinking hastily.

Dakota stood tense on the side of the road, leaning against a metal banister, frowning as she willed her phone to connect faster.

She'd have to get a ride and break every speed limit there was.

Was she second-guessing herself?

Or was she following her gut?

She huffed in frustration as she glanced at the horizon, watching the sun dip. And then, her phone connected, and she felt a prickle down her spine.

They were running out of time, and now Marcus and Dakota were heading in opposite directions.

"H-hello?" she said slowly, wincing against a sudden blare of a horn from the opposite side of the road. "This is Agent Dakota Steele, BAU. I need a ride. Yes, yes, I can verify. One second."

CHAPTER TWENTY SEVEN

Dakota's hair whipped about her face and the sirens wailed above her, the red and blue lights flashing against the evening sky. The night had fallen now, pushing the sun back into its nocturnal hiding spot.

The state trooper kept glancing at her, but she didn't look back. The man had insisted they keep the windows down, since the air conditioning was broken. He'd also insisted on playing heavy metal over the radio, drumming his fingers against the steering wheel along with the sound.

He'd nearly done a U-turn to help pursue a speeder towards the start of the trip but Dakota had put her foot down and he'd reluctantly stayed the course.

And now, ahead, she spotted the large pharmaceutical lab set against the desert backdrop. Large sand dunes like whale humps in an ocean arose from the otherwise desolate terrain. Strange, scrubby, scraggy plants pockmarked the ground.

The cop veered up towards the security gates, waving towards them. "See," he said in a drawling tone. "Like I said—place is sealed tighter than a hooker's—"

Dakota cleared her throat, interrupting him and pointing off towards a parking spot just inside the gate. "See any way to access the..." she trailed off, frowning. Then shot a quick look towards her driver. "Sirens off, please," she said quickly. "Don't want to alert him."

The patrolman took his time about it but nodded, flicking a silver switch on the dash. The siren stopped. The flashing blue and red lights went suddenly still. Dakota frowned through the windshield, eyes on the large building ahead. As the evening fell, a slow chill came across the desert, and now the wind moving through the window carried the odd tinge of warmth from stale air, ushered in seconds later by a chilly breeze gusting over the uninterrupted desert.

The officer pulled up to the gate, but the metal blockade remained motionless. No one sat in the guardhouse, and Dakota frowned, tugging uncomfortably at her fight-scarred ear. She could feel the officer eyeing the tattoos along her wrist, curious, but she tugged at her sleeves and pushed out of the vehicle, standing outside the pharmaceutical lab.

She glanced at her phone. Nearly seven p.m. The place was closed now. She peered in the direction of a multi-level, concrete parking lot. No sign of vehicles... A couple of cars were parked just inside the gate, suggesting that some stragglers or security officers still lingered behind.

Dakota peered in the direction of the main building. She spotted some movement on a lower level, behind large windows.

She frowned, and said, "Mind doing me a favor?"

"I have orders to assist in any way I can. Backup should be here in a few minutes."

Dakota hesitated. She glanced once more towards the window, and the moving figures. She said, "I don't think we have time to wait."

He frowned at her, tipping the brim of his wide, leather hat. "I'm afraid I can't assist until backup has arrived."

She hesitated, glancing once more out the window. And then, she let out a sudden huff of air. "All right. If you can't come with me, stay here. Tell them where I went. If you don't hear back from me in a few minutes, send them in"

She didn't wait to argue but instead, pushed out of the vehicle, and hurried forward, approaching the gate. A large, concrete wall circled the compound. She peered through the bars at the guard house, making sure no one was slumbering within and then, with a faint puff of air, she gripped the bars, and began to climb.

Dakota had always been good at pull-ups. Her training, when she'd been a fighter, had incorporated all sorts of physically demanding movements. Now, her muscles strained, and she could feel the friction against her hands from the rigid bars.

She let out a puff of air, wincing as she used her feet to wedge between the bars.

She clambered up the surface of the gate, reached the top, avoiding jutting metal protrusions shaped like ornate spearheads, and pulled herself gingerly over. She perched for a second on top of the gate, and glanced back towards the cop still sitting in the vehicle. She gave him a long look.

He didn't move, preferring to watch, his headlights illuminating the cold metal beneath her.

She let out a long sigh of resignation. She would have to wait for backup to arrive to get any help from the state trooper.

But there was no time to wait.

She gingerly avoided the metal protrusions, and then scaled the other side of the gate, dropping the last few feet and landing nimbly; she dusted her hands off, rolling her fingers and letting out a satisfied grunt.

Then, with a nod towards the police car, she turned, and broke into a jog, heading in the direction of the cars she'd seen, as well as the movement inside the building behind the large windows.

As she hastened forward, breathing heavily, she felt her phone vibrate.

She tensed, wondering if the state trooper was trying to contact her. But then she pulled her phone and recognized the number.

She reached the parked vehicles and came to a halt behind them, her eyes darting along the license plates. "Hello?" she answered the call.

"Dakota," said Marcus. "I'm here. It's not him."

"Wait, what? You're sure?"

"Pretty sure. He's in custody, now. His dad showed up with a lawyer. But Tommy Barrett has video footage of himself sitting in one of his old professor's offices, secretly recording."

Dakota wrinkled her nose. "Pardon?"

"I've only made it through a part of the video, but by the sound of things he was trying to trap the professor into admitting that he lowered his grade. Regardless, the video was recorded while Ms. Childs was attacked. It's not Tommy. His alibi is solid. There's even a clock visible in the background of the professor's office. It matches the phone's timestamp."

Dakota felt a strange tingle along her spine. Just because it wasn't Mr. Barrett, didn't automatically mean that it was Moore. But still, her eyes moved along the cars, towards the window. She said, slowly, "I need to run some license plates."

"Shoot."

Dakota quickly read off the plates outside the main building. There were only three cars.

Marcus took a second, and then he said, "None of those belong to Moore or any of his known associates."

Dakota bit her lip. She knew now, that either she had made a horrible mistake, or Tyler was somewhere nearby. "Alright, keep me posted."

"Hang on," Marcus said urgently, "Where are you? I'm watching police bulletins—I don't see any units at that facility yet."

"They're a few steps behind," she said through pressed teeth. "Don't worry about it."

"Like hell I won't. That's the one thing I'm good at, Dakota, worrying on your behalf when you refuse to."

"I'm just looking around for now."

"Can you wait?" Marcus let out a long breath. "Never mind, stupid question. I forgot who I was speaking to. I'm on my way."

Dakota hesitated. He was nearly an hour away. There was no way he could arrive in time. But it didn't matter. She had to keep looking. If Tyler Moore was anywhere nearby, she would have to stop him herself.

She gave a quick farewell, stowed her phone, double checking that it was on silent, and then began to hastily move towards the window.

She arrived at a small entrance that led to what looked like a cafeteria. She spotted long rectangular tables, with neat, cushioned seats. The office version of a school lunch table.

She tried the door handle but it wouldn't open. She huffed in frustration and tried again, rattling the lock. She tugged at the handle, trying to open the door.

She spotted the silhouettes just inside the glass moving, and heard the sound of voices.

One of the figures hastened towards the door, and she thought she glimpsed the sudden beam of a flashlight.

She raised a hand cautiously but her other hand landed near the holster of her weapon.

In the raised hand, she was already carrying her ID.

There was a buzzing sound, the lock above the door flashed green and then, slowly, the door opened.

A man wearing a blue uniform, with a shoulder mic, was staring at her. He blinked, and she said, "Agent Dakota Steele, FBI."

He hesitated, shaking his head, and muttering, "You can't be–what are–I don't think–"

Dakota glanced past him at the older women wearing lab coats sitting at the table, their legs crossed, their hands resting on their knees. One of them had a laptop open in front of her, and the other was sipping on a steaming mug of what smelled like coffee.

Both of them glanced towards the door, frowning in the direction of the disturbance.

"I need all three of you to leave," Dakota said firmly. "It's not safe for you here."

At these words, the two women and the man who looked like the security guard, all stiffened.

One of the women, who was at the laptop, said, "And why should we do that?"

Dakota brushed past the security guard. He tried to grab her wrist, but she easily avoided the grasp as she said, "We have reason to believe your lives might be in danger. There's a suspected fugitive who was heading towards this location. We think he's already on the premises."

"Dawkins?" the same woman said, glancing towards the man. "Did anyone come through?"

The other woman lowered her steaming coffee mug and muttered, 'What's the point of a security guard if he's not at the gate?"

Dakota said, firmly, "If I can climb the fence, someone else could."

The security guard looked astonished. "You *climbed* the fence?" he demanded, his eyes narrowed.

Dakota looked him dead in the eyes. "Focus, please. I need you to take these women, get in your cars, and leave." Dakota glanced the table. "If you're working, take it with you. I'm sorry, but backup is on its way, and I don't have time to explain this to you. Please, go."

All the while, she kept her badge raised, as some sort of amplifier.

The guard still looked perturbed about her comment concerning climbing the gates. But the two women were shifting uncomfortably, murmuring, and then slowly packing their things.

Dakota stepped aside, and didn't move until the two women had finally exited the door, and approached the vehicles in the parking lot.

The guard himself muttered a couple of times, and shot Dakota a look as the vehicles began to move.

Dakota nodded towards the gate. "They're going to need you to let them through."

The man frowned at her, adjusting the microphone on his lapel. He hitched his belt, the flashlight which he had turned off now swaying in a loop of fabric. "I'm not able to let you just wander around aimlessly. You need to come with me."

Dakota shook her head firmly.

The guard began to protest, but she said, "You had better let those two out."

And then without further comment, she began to move, hastening through the building, towards the first flight of stairs she had seen.

This would have been far easier with two people, or more. But Marcus wasn't here. The patrolman was waiting for backup, and backup was still a few minutes away.

There was no telling where the killer was.

So, with a frustrated sigh, but a determined stride, she hastened towards the stairs, taking them three at a time. The security guard tried to protest again, but she was ignoring him.

For now, she had more important things to worry about. Eventually, she heard the sound of the door buzzing shut.

As she reached the second floor landing, she glanced through a window, spotting the guard jogging to his position to open the gate for the two sedans attempting to leave.

Now, there was only one other vehicle in the parking lot, and this one she guessed belonged to the guard himself.

She hesitated, scanning the hall that led from the second floor foyer through the heart of the building.

She held her breath for a moment, waiting.

But there was no movement. No sign of anything. No sound, and no flash of light.

She hesitated for a second, glancing towards the stairs. And then, she broke into a run; she would have to make this quick. She didn't have time to search every room of every floor.

She hastened along the second floor hallway, picking up the pace. But no matter where she glanced, the doors were either shut or rooms empty.

No lights beneath the doors, no suggestion that anyone was *here*.

She reached the end of the hall, and still running, breathing heavily now, taking the stairs to the third floor.

And like this, faster, faster, she desperately swiveled her head side to side, looking for anything out of place, anything that might catch the eye.

CHAPTER TWENTY EIGHT

The chemist smiled, staring across the dark space. Concrete columns segmented the structure and he spotted where the car door slammed. She was moving slowly, adjusting her purse

She always came in late. Her boyfriend worked as a security guard at the company.

He had known this as well.

He felt a faint chill of air, and he moved slowly. He had parked behind the building, far enough away that no one had seen him; an unsupervised garage off from the main campus.

Now, he picked up his pace, moving as quietly as he could while also closing the distance.

His footsteps thumped against the floor.

He could hear her, now, murmuring to herself. "Come on, Jamie, pick up."

She shook the phone in one hand. She had such delicate hands.

Those were not the hands of a chemist. They were not the hands of someone who spent time in the lab, and yet this was the bitch who had taken his job. This was the person they had replaced him with.

He felt a flash of rage, and he couldn't help but run faster. Fifteen feet, ten, closing the distance. But his footsteps pounded against the concrete now.

She tensed, and began to turn.

She rounded on him, and it took a second as he closed the distance for her eyes to widen in horrified realization.

A scream caught on her lips, but his hand moved to stop it.

The sound was muffled, and he brought her crashing down, with him on top.

She hit the concrete with a loud *thump*. His arm and knee struck as well. Pain lanced up his body, but he kept his position, pinning her to the floor.

He breathed in sharp, desperate gasps for air.

She tried to shout; tried to bite his finger. He cursed, yanking his hand back. "Get off me!" she yelled. But he laughed in her face.

"No one is going to hear you scream," he whispered fiercely in her ear.

Her eyes widened in terror, and she continued to struggle.

She inhaled deeply, trying to scream once more, but again, he clapped his hand over her mouth. He didn't hold her to the floor; instead, muscles straining, breath coming in gasps, he yanked her to her feet.

She struggled, but there was nothing she could do. He reached for her purse, yanking it, and ripping the car keys from the compartment where he had watched her store them.

As she continued to fight, to shove at his hands, he yanked the key from the purse, and clicked it.

The lights to the vehicle flashed.

And then he hit her.

She was still fighting, though, refusing to give in.

He hit her again, and she stopped struggling.

Breathing heavily, he reached for the door handle, yanking the car door open. And then he shoved her into the vehicle.

This was the perfect spot for what he had planned. In a way, the only spot. The most appropriate location for his vengeance.

They had humiliated him.

It took him a few motions to heft a live body into the car. He was gasping, sweaty by the time he had deposited her limp figure, then slammed the door shut.

He let out a heavy sigh, wiping his hand across his forehead. He clicked the locks again, and this time they flashed.

He put the keys in his pocket, and began to pace hastily back towards his own vehicle. Back towards where he had kept his metal lunchbox and the precious thermos with his new project.

He was determined to see it through.

He shot a look back over his shoulder, frowning towards the vehicle.

No motion. He could just about to glimpse her head jutting over the dashboard, visible through the windshield.

An expensive car.

"Did daddy buy that for you?" he muttered beneath his breath, feeling a flash of resentment.

He reached his vehicle, flung open the door, and reached for the metal lunchbox on the ground.

He paused, inhaling slowly, forcing his nerves to calm.

If he wanted this to succeed, he couldn't rush. In fact, he was determined to savor the moment. It had taken him nearly a year to create this new concoction, but it had also taken him a year to plan all of this.

What came next was going to be the best part yet. He had promised the police two more bodies by tonight.

He chuckled slowly, and reached for the container.

He slammed the door, not bothering to be quiet about it. The only other person who usually stayed this late was her boyfriend, and he rarely stayed in the guardhouse, preferring to do rounds in the larger building.

Besides, she was early. Normally, they didn't rendezvous until eight. But it was their anniversary. And she had wanted to surprise him. That was why she had worn the red underwear. He smiled, confident he had discovered everything he needed to in order to succeed. He didn't know how the sheep made it through life bleating at the stupidest things.

By the end of the night, they would know just how foolish they'd been. He nodded to himself, feeling the faint tremor in his hand which he ignored. Fear was beneath him. Nervousness was for the weak.

He grabbed the thermos, slammed his door, clicked the locks. As he marched away, he thought how silly this last gesture had been.

He didn't need the locks. He didn't need his car. In fact, he was never going to drive again.

***

Dakota was gasping heavily now, the sweat streaming down her face. Through the top floor window, eight stories high, she stared out, and watched a cavalcade of police and emergency vehicles racing down the highway, heading in her direction.

Backup had nearly arrived.

But it was a waste. He wasn't here.

She had checked every floor. She hadn't managed to look in every single office, but now she was beginning to wonder if she ought to go back and do just this.

She took a moment to lean against the window, both arms outstretched, touching the chilled glass. She exhaled deeply.

And then she spotted a flash of light.

She frowned.

Another flash of light.

Briefly, she wondered if someone was setting off small fireworks.

But then she realized where the light was coming from.

She stared.

The parking garage she had spotted on the way in. It was set off from the main building, outside the gate.

She hadn't even considered the parking garage. In her excitement, she'd failed to pay attention to the squat structure beyond the wall.

But now, she stared towards the third level of it.

The flashing lights had been nearly unnoticeable.

And now the lights were dead.

She hesitated, inhaling shakily. Already exhausted, having sprinted upstairs, rushing down hallways, she felt a flicker of lethargy.

But with a resigned sigh, shooting one last glance towards the stream of emergency vehicles racing towards her, she broke into a sprint again, rushing back out of the office door, into the hall, and down the stairs.

CHAPTER TWENTY NINE

Dakota reached the third floor of the garage, and her legs were like rubber; she nearly toppled as she stumbled up the ramp.

Her eyes were fixed on the single vehicle in the place.

The license plate had been removed.

She frowned at the green sedan. The car matched the description of Tyler Moore's vehicle.

She tensed, letting out only a whisper of a breath. Her weapon slowly emerged, and she gripped it tightly

She didn't speak, didn't make a sound, as she slowly moved into the garage, glancing one way, then the other.

And that's when she spotted it; a second vehicle beyond the concrete column.

She frowned, staring, and she could feel her heart racing, the sweat from running and sprinting and taking the stairs turning to a cold glaze along her skin.

She reached up, brushing her hair out of her face, taking another step for a better look around the concrete column.

And then she froze.

"Drop it!" she yelled.

A figure went stiff. He was standing near the back window of the second vehicle, something gripped tightly in his hands.

"Don't you dare move!" she said, her voice hoarse.

The man was wearing something strapped to his face. She could only see the back of his head now, though, so she wasn't able to determine what he was wearing.

"Hands up, I mean it!"

He was still pressing something against the window. "She's fine," said a voice. It was a muffled, effeminate voice.

The figure standing by the window was distinctly male but his voice was soft, lilting.

"Tyler?" she said, hesitantly.

He fidgeted uncomfortably.

"Tyler Moore?" she said more firmly.

Sometimes, with people like this, it was enough to unmask them with words.

But he didn't turn to look at her.

"Police?" he said slowly.

She realized he was watching her reflection off the glass of the vehicle's window. She took a hesitant, cautious step to the left.

"I mean it," she insisted. "If you move I'll shoot; get your hands away from that window."

"I told you, she's fine, for now. But," he said in that effeminate voice, "you shoot me, it won't go so well for her."

Dakota swallowed, her throat hoarse. "What do you mean?"

She could hear sirens now, approaching.

She thought she glimpsed the flash of red and blue lights off the large building across from the parking garage.

"Too late," he said slowly.

"What did you do?" she demanded.

Only then did he slowly turn, hands raised limply. He stared at her, his face revealing a strange brass and rubber thing; his mouth was concealed but his eyes were just about visible behind the streaked and smudged glass.

He stared at her, and shook a finger in front of his face. In his other hand, he clutched a silver thermos.

"I was working on activating this," he said. "I managed to get my hands on some before I was canned from this place..."

Dakota felt a strange shiver up her spine at the sound of his voice.

There was no fear; he was facing the barrel of a gun, but he didn't seem afraid. "Do you want to know what this is?" he said in a singsong voice, smiling at her.

Dakota hesitated. She felt confident the answer was no, but at the same time, if he was talking, it meant he was occupied.

She took another step to the side, trying to get a new angle to look into the front seat of the second car.

She thought she spotted the head of a figure.

The head was moving, groggily, slowly. A hand lifted, gingerly pressing against the figure's forehead.

Tyler shot a look over his shoulder, still wearing that horrible gas mask. "Looks like she's waking," he murmured. He stared back. "I used to work here, you know?"

She frowned at him.

He continued, "They said I was unstable; it was the reason I underperformed in that class but they shouldn't have expelled me."

"You poisoned your teacher."

He smiled at her. "I suppose there's no harm in affirming that. I did.

He had it coming, though."

Dakota said, "What do you plan to do with her?"

"Haven't you seen my other projects?"

Dakota still wasn't sure if she could take the clean shot. For the moment, he was standing staring right at her, completely exposed. Then again, she wasn't sure if anyone was in immediate danger. The way he was holding that metal thermos, though, made her skin tingle. "What is that?" she redirected once more.

He wiggled the container, laughing. "A masterpiece; I did the best work they had here. My ideas were brilliant. I would have made it far, if not for tampering." He sneered, and shot another look over his shoulder at the woman in the car. "She thought she could take my job. But it's mine. And I'm here to take back something she wants to keep."

Dakota scowled. "Why don't you put that thermos on the ground, and back away from the car."

She could hear shouting now. Slamming doors and flashing lights.

Tyler grinned at her. "Sounds like we have an audience. Good; I want everyone to see this."

She felt another prickle as she took a hesitant step towards him now, her finger still taught against the trigger.

He shook his head though, the brass components of the gas mask swaying. "Careful, you don't want to get too close... Then again, it won't matter."

"What did you do?"

"This," he said slowly, "is the very first of its kind. Do you know how rare it is to find a *first* of anything?" He gave another little chuckle. "I created it. Me. On my own. None of them helped. How could they? How could any of you? You don't understand what I'm doing. You don't understand who you're dealing with, do you?"

"Why don't you explain it to me."

He started at her. "Does a wolf owe an explanation to a lamb?"

Dakota didn't say anything, wondering if she ought to just risk the shot. She wasn't sure what was in that container of his, but she felt confident that she didn't want anyone to find out.

"This," he said importantly, "is the very first synthetically manufactured pathogen of its kind." He beamed, his eyes widening behind the gas mask.

Dakota hesitated. "What sort of pathogen?"

He nodded, in approval. "I'm glad you asked, and I'm excited to share it with the world. I've worked on this project for a very long time, but be warned—If you shoot me, the lid will release. I hope you know

141

that."

He seemed to be reading her intentions.

She took another step forward.

He glared at her from behind the glass. "This is my own cocktail. Do you know how many strands of the common cold there are?" He was smirking again. She could hear it in his voice. "As a chemist, I'm not normally or particularly interested in biological weapons. But this isn't a weapon so much as a work of art. To synthetically manufacture this took a genius that is staggering. You can't possibly comprehend what I did... The cold is so mutated that increasing the danger of it will serve as a second culling event!"

Dakota took another step forward.

She didn't quite understand everything he was saying. To her, some of it sounded like word salad, trying to act impressive.

She slowly holstered her weapon, though, deciding if she couldn't risk shooting him, maybe she could help calm him down.

In response, he reached up, grabbed at his mask, and pulled it slowly down.

He had a round, pockmarked face. His eyes were narrowed and his nose was slightly pig-like, turned up, and large.

He had clever eyes that stared out at her.

She could feel her heart pounding and was now within a few steps of him.

"Go ahead," he murmured. "Shoot me. I dare you."

Dakota left her weapon in her holster now; if what he was saying was true, she couldn't risk allowing him to drop that thermos.

But also, he had let her close the distance. This was something she noticed often about men who targeted women. There was something of an epidemic of underestimation.

Most men didn't like to think that a woman could kick their ass.

But now, only a few feet away, her weapon holstered, she watched a man with a shit-eating grin.

She said, "Last chance."

Moore frowned at her. "What are you, stupid? Didn't you hear me?" he said with a sneer. "If you don't leave now, I'm going to open this thermos, and release –"

She kicked, hard.

The same kick she had used with the lighter back in the room full of gasoline.

Her foot hit his wrist. His hand went limp as he shouted.

The thermos went into the air.

He screamed, his face twisting in rage like a petulant child throwing a temper tantrum. He lunged at her, trying to shove her out of the way so the thermos would fall.

But she was already moving. The thermos needed a soft landing spot.

So she hit him in the throat, if only to keep him distracted.

He let out a choking, gargling sound, clutching at his neck.

At the same time, she ripped the front of his shirt forward, pulling on the ample fabric, and stretching it

The thermos landed right where she stretched the shirt, bouncing off the fabric.

She caught it with her other hand.

Immediately, she twisted at the lid, making sure it was secure. Moore was still screeching, in between gagging, choking sounds.

But using both her hands to check the lid had cost her precious time.

He came crashing down on her, shoving her to the floor.

One advantage he did have was sheer size.

She kept a grip on the thermos as if it were a football, and her head swung back, hard, striking the concrete.

She let out a faint, strangled gasp. Dark spots flashed across her eyes.

Tyler was gasping, grunting as he struggled for the thermos.

But she pulled it out of his reach. She kicked, shoving him off her.

He got one look at her, eyes wide in horror, and then, instead of going for his precious thermos a second time, he spun and rushed back towards the car.

The keys were in his hand. The locks *clicked*. The lights flashed.

She could hear the sound of police officers now on the ramp leading up to the parking level. Obviously, they had heard something, or were simply fanning out in order to find her.

But too late. He got into the vehicle, jamming the keys in the ignition.

She was already moving, taking a split second to consider her options. If she dove behind one of the concrete columns, she would be safe. There was no way Moore could get away. But on the other hand, there was a woman trapped in that car with him. She didn't doubt what would happen to her, if the vehicle was peppered with bullets.

And the police were on edge. A car screeching towards them at full speed would only tempt their trigger fingers.

And so Dakota lunged forward. Her gun in her hand. The car began to back up, tires squealing as he floored the pedal.

She shot twice, breaking the back *and* front windshield.

He ducked, though. She hadn't been aiming low enough to hit him, either way. She didn't want to risk shooting the victim.

The car swerved as he attempted to slam it into her, but she darted to the side, avoiding the screeching vehicle.

As it sped towards her, squealing, and leaving rubber against the ground, she shot two of the tires.

The vehicle now hit one of the barriers, unable to redirect momentum fast enough; metal scraped against concrete—chips of the material went flying. Smoke was now pouring from the back of the car. But the front window was shattered where she had shot it.

And she came charging forward now, stopping long enough to snatch something off the ground: a hefty, part-brass gas mask.

Moore was cursing. Gone was the cocksure attitude. Gone was the self-contented smirk. He sat in a stained seat amidst shards of glass.

And then he shot a look towards Dakota, snarling; he floored the pedal again. This time heading forward, trying to hit her a second time.

She flung the gas mask, like a baseball.

She didn't want to risk shooting the woman, who was still groggily getting to a sitting position. But her makeshift projectile, topped by the heavy brass filter, collided with Moore. His head snapped back, and he made a loud gasping sound.

Dakota was able to jump on top of the moving vehicle. It hadn't picked up enough speed to cause harm. She rolled across the hood, moving towards where Tyler was shaking his head, cursing. He was bleeding from his brow now, and still furious.

She grabbed him by the scruff of the shirt she had used to catch his thermos. She was still holding his precious cargo in her other hand.

She resisted the urge to hit him with the thermos, but pulled him, bodily from the front of the car, over the shattered glass, onto the hood.

The car rolled slowly to a halt.

She could hear the loud shouting of police. The sound of desperate voices. Megaphones. The whir of sirens.

Tyler Moore was gasping, trying to tear at her fingers, to rip her off him.

But she refused to let go.

"Stop moving," she snapped, breathing heavily.

She lowered the thermos next to her, and then reached for her handcuffs, fingers shaking.

She turned Tyler onto his stomach, pressing him against the hood of his vehicle. And then, with still shaking hands, breathing desperately in the gray, concrete garage, she began—

A *click.*

Then a *hiss.*

Suddenly, Dakota felt a puff of mist against her chin. She blinked, frowning, glancing down. And then she realized... She'd crushed something against Moore's chest. He was breathing heavily, staring up at her, blood still streaming down his forehead, but his cheeks had now twisted into a leer.

"Whoops," he whispered.

It took her a second to notice the small shards of glass in his chest pocket. A plastic, orange cap had fallen down his abdomen, onto the hood of the car.

She stared, not quite comprehending.

And then, a cold shiver of horror welled up inside her.

"Whoopsie," he repeated, giggling now. "Did you really think you could best *me*?"

The police were shouting. Footsteps were thumping.

Dakota tried to yell a warning. But her lips were suddenly numb. She tried to maintain her grip on Moore, but her fingers began to slip.

"I have a tolerance against it," he whispered. "An inoculation of my own design..."

She suddenly slipped off the edge of the car, but her legs wouldn't support her weight.

She toppled to the ground, head hitting the floor painfully. But as she tried to move, to rise, to blink... *nothing.* She was frozen. Motionless.

Helpless.

He was still giggling as he stared down at her, slipping off the hood of the car. She spotted silhouettes behind her now. But Moore stooped, reaching for her holster, withdrawing her weapon. She tried to stave off his fingers, but her own hand was rigid now.

And then she realized...

Paralytic.

That was what the coroner had said.

The killer used a paralytic first to subdue his victims.

She'd crushed a vial of the chemical by accident—or design? Had he intended this?

It didn't matter. Shouting now, above her.

"Back away! Back away! I'll kill her! I'll do it! Get the hell back!"

She watched as Moore reached out for the metal thermos. He was

145

breathing heavily now, hyperventilating. He faced multiple police officers who continued to spill up the ramp, all of them pointing their weapons at Moore.

"I said get back!" he screamed. "I'll splatter the ground with her brains! I mean it! Don't test me! This—this is a bomb!" he screamed, waving the thermos around above his head.

Dakota winced... A bomb? He'd said it was some sort of plague earlier...

And then she felt a jolt of humiliation... He'd been lying. He'd tricked her, hadn't he? He'd been trying to kill the woman in the car, but she hadn't known what to expect.

And now she lay with wavering consciousness on the ground. Moore still gripped his thermos, and the police were holding their fire.

Another flutter of Dakota's eyelashes, a faint murmur.

And then her consciousness flitted away.

CHAPTER THIRTY

Dakota eyes fluttered again, and she let out a faint groan. She tried to shift, but realized her surroundings were zipping by. She swallowed, letting out a faint gasp of air, blinking and trying to make sense of her surroundings.

Her arm brushed against skin.

She jolted, and tried to turn, but her head moved so slowly. Her fingers tensed, but didn't quite uncurl. She shot a slow look in the direction of the figure reclining next to her.

A young woman with curling brown hair and horn-rimmed glasses. She was similarly leaning back, eyes half-closed as if in some sort of trance or slumber.

Dakota tried to speak, but her tongue felt as if it were glued to the roof of her mouth. She tried to sit up fully, but it took an exertion of her core muscles that left her feeling sore.

Her head jolted, bouncing off a window.

And then she realized she was sitting in the backseat of the car. The desert terrain outside the pharmaceutical lab flashed past. The car was speeding. Bright lights shone ahead of the vehicle, illuminating the road... But no...

An even brighter light than the vehicle's headlights.

It took Dakota a second to realize what it was... But then she heard the faint *whump-whump* of helicopter blades. She stiffened.

"No, no," the man driving the car was whispering. Moore was wearing his gas mask again, his voice muffled. His thermos sat on the seat next to him. "Doesn't *have* to be me, does it?" he muttered. "I can give them *two*. This was fate... No such thing as fate. But this... this was my genius. I didn't even know it. She can be the second." He nodded to himself hurriedly, hands gripping the steering wheel so tightly Dakota thought he was trying to strangle it.

His eyes darted to the rearview mirror. He stared out from his smudged mask, and his eyes were only just visible in the bright lights across the hood of the car. "Hello," he said, cheerfully. "You're my new volunteer. Lucky you." He chuckled, and put on an extra burst of speed.

Dakota's head thumped against the window again as she was jostled where she reclined in the back seat. Her eyes were blinking quicker now, her fingers could curl and uncurl. Which meant the tranquilizer he'd used was slowly, so *very* slowly, wearing off.

Moore was shaking his head. "You know!" he shouted now, over his shoulder, "I was going to do the unthinkable... To deprive this universe of *my* mind! Ha!" He shook his head his gas mask swaying. "Can you imagine?" He snorted. "How silly of me... but no, no... just more societal conditioning. Self-sacrifice isn't *noble*. There is no such thing as nobility. Not *really*."

Dakota tried to speak, her limbs numb. But she managed to eke out, "Tu-urn yourself in." She had to gasp to draw in more air after even this small amount of speech. "It isn't worth it. Just turn yourself in!"

He was giggling now, his fingers still glued to the steering wheel. "You can be my second... Yes... I—I have plans. Bigger plans. And you," he shot a look over his shoulder again, snorting in derision. "How stupid can you be? A plague? A common cold—haha! What do I look like a dirty virologist?"

Dakota didn't reply now, her eyes darting out the window. She spotted the beam of light from the helicopter following them. In the rearview mirror, she also spotted red and blue flashing as police vehicles followed as well.

She supposed Moore must have bluffed his way out of the car garage as well. Or, perhaps, he'd simply threatened to shoot the two women.

"No," he said simply, "This," he tapped his fingers against his cannister, "will kill you both. *Very* slowly. Very painfully. It's a masterpiece. Trust me, one day, the U.S. government is going to beg me for my help." He nodded adamantly. "And just imagine," he added, his voice shaking now. "You thought you could take *my job!*" he screamed now, directing his ire towards the second figure in the back.

Dakota's mind was desperately spinning, struggling to think of some way out of this situation. He had her weapon. She could see it sitting in his lap. He had the thermos—whatever was in that. And he was heading up dusty, desert roads in some unknown direction.

The helicopter continued to pursue, but he didn't seem too concerned with this.

He chuckled, shooting a look at Dakota. "I told them I had a bomb. They believed me too. Shouldn't there be some sort of IQ test to join the FBI? I mean... dumb cops, I get it. But dumb agents too?" He made a gagging sound. "Enough to make anyone sick."

Dakota's fingers were now able to curl and uncurl. She didn't have a weapon on her. It was clear that this man was some type of egomaniac.

Being perceived as intelligent clearly mattered to him.

A *lot.*

But she wasn't the one trained in talking psychotics down from their plans. For her, using her fists was the more effective strategy. Some people just weren't worth reasoning with.

Marcus was the talker...

But he was still a half hour away, at least.

Shit. She thought desperately.

She tried to think what to say, but her mind was drawing a blank. Everything was still hazy, foggy. She let out a frustrated sigh. The killer was still ranting, talking about his genius. Talking about just how clever he'd been.

Dakota didn't really care to listen; her fingers were now in her pocket, still moving slowly. She'd completely regained the use of her hand, though. Her arm, however, was still prickling, limp, under the influence of whatever cocktail of drugs he'd used on her.

She pulled her phone out surreptitiously, feeling for the glass to know which direction to slide it up her body so the killer wouldn't see.

He was still shooting nervous glances into the mirrors every now and then, but he seemed confident. He was saying, "I'd say another ten minutes before you can move... And then..." He chuckled. "Then I'm going to have to do something *really* fun. I've never shot at cops before. Do you think I'll take one? Two?" he shook his head. "Or... There's a tunnel through a mountain about fifteen miles from here. Could lose them, couldn't I? Could leave your bodies behind, rotting for them to find." He giggled. "So many fun options, aren't there?"

Dakota was barely listening. She'd managed to navigate the phone to her shoulder now. She glanced down, trying not to let the light flash out and catch his attention. He still had her gun. Still was driving the car at a breakneck pace. Neither Dakota nor the woman next to her were wearing seatbelts.

As she navigated her phone, though, she was grateful Marcus was on speed dial. She entered his number and then waited, listening as the phone tried to connect.

It did after only one ring.

"Dakota?" his voice exclaimed, loud.

She winced, quickly, with trembling fingers trying to lower the volume.

"What was that?" Moore snapped.

Dakota faked as if she were coughing, hoping he was too distracted to notice. Moore was watching the helicopter though, eyes fixated front.

She felt a faint prickle of sweat on her forehead and shifted uncomfortably, swallowing and tasting salt on her lips. The weight of the phone against her shoulder shifted as she tried to twist her chin in such a way to further hide it from view.

The sirens behind them were wailing now. The chopper blades above continued to pulse.

But with killers like this, who had already determined suicide as an option, she had to be very delicate; the police didn't have the same information she did. The helicopter above was not apprised to the killer's psychology.

She'd lowered the volume now. The killer distracted again. The woman next to Dakota was glancing over, her eyes widening in horror. She shifted uncomfortably in the seat, staring at Dakota, and giving short, jerking shakes of her head.

But Dakota couldn't afford to accommodate the woman's fear.

Not now. Dakota's own terror came in the form of pins and needles up her back. Her elbow scraped the smooth, leather lining of the door. Her cheek pressed against the window.

Then, trying to time her words in relation to where the killer was looking, she said, "You really do think you're some type of genius, is that right?"

She was addressing the killer but she spoke with her mouth angled, hoping desperately that Marcus was paying close attention.

"What do you think?" he snapped. "I mean, look at you. Look at *her*," he said. "You're some type of agent, and she's supposed to be a hotshot, a rising star at the pharmaceutical lab."

He chuckled. He shook his head, and shrugged. "I guess that makes me better than both of you, doesn't it?"

She could hear heavy breathing on the phone. She was nodding along with the killer's words, trying not to rile him up

Then, through the muted speakers, the volume so low she could barely pick out the words, "Is that him?" Marcus said.

"Yes," Dakota said loudly, "I can tell, you're very smart. And that matters to you a lot. Is that why you've been killing people? Because of how clever you are?"

She could hear Marcus on the line still. She didn't want to direct the killer's attention. But she also didn't have an infinite amount of time. He had said something about ten minutes before the drugs wore off completely and he had to make a choice. Not long at all. So she said, "Maybe you could tell me what to say—what do you want to hear?"

This she directed again towards Moore. He didn't seem to realize she was speaking to someone else.

He snorted. "Too late for any of that. You should've led with it. Maybe I would've allowed you to live if you had shown the proper respect. But no, even then. I don't need your respect. I don't need any of you. I've been thinking about this moment for so long. I've always known I would have a special destiny. I've always felt it."

Dakota just nodded, allowing him to continue to talk. He seemed to like doing a lot of this.

Now, though, Agent Clement seemed to have caught on. "You need to play this one of two ways," Marcus rattled off, his words coming quickly, "Dear God, Dakota, listen closely, please..." he trailed off, his voice thick with emotion, but then, just as quickly, professional as ever, Marcus said, "You can either align with him as an ally, or submit to him as some fan. He doesn't want your admiration. He wants your worship, but if you give it to him, he'll kill you. Once he has what he wants, he won't see any use for you."

Dakota tried to listen. Marcus was the one who had done negotiation training. He had specialized in psychology and trained in abnormal psychology. This was his area of expertise. Plus, Dakota secretly believed that most people didn't have the same emotional intelligence as her partner. Growing up, Dakota had often considered herself a woman of action... not words.

Marcus was still talking, "Ask him about his previous victims. Compliment him on the murders."

She could hear the shaking in her partner's voice as he issued the instruction. She felt a similar distaste. Her stomach turning. But if that was what the moment required, then that was what she would do.

"I saw what you did to the others," she said, her voice still rasping. Her lips still prickly. Whatever paralytic he had used hadn't yet worn off. "I was impressed. It was very..." she struggled for words, and ended with, "*impressive*."

Marcus whispered into the phone, "Ask him if he thinks there's anyone else who could have done the same."

Dakota said, "You think there's someone as smart as you? I've heard of others that could do similar things."

Tyler Moore snorted. "Don't be ridiculous. There's no one like me. When have you ever heard of someone like me?"

She hesitated, shifting uncomfortably. "He poisoned his professor," said Marcus quietly, "tell him that Oppenheimer did the same."

Dakota said, "Oppenheimer did the same."

"What?"

She winced, realizing she hadn't added the full comment. "Oppenheimer also poisoned his professor," she said. "He helped create a nuclear bomb that took out two cities."

Now he was staring into the rearview mirror, glaring at her; she kept her chin angled to the side, her shoulder hunched, still trying to disguise the phone.

He looked angrier now. The helicopter was still flying above them, the police cars behind them were closing the distance, slowly. Dakota could feel a rising sense of uncertainty. One way or another, it was all going to end soon.

"You think Oppenheimer is better than me?" he snapped.

"Ask him to prove he's not," Marcus said urgently. "Offer to help."

Dakota said, "Maybe I can help. I think you're better than him. I definitely think you're better. I just don't know if anyone else will. If you get yourself killed now," she said, slowly, trying to think what he would want her to say. "Then no one will imagine what you could do with another ten years, fifty."

He was still red-faced, flustered. But now he was nodding slowly as if this made sense. "You're not wrong," he said. He scoffed. "Though I definitely don't need your help."

Dakota shrugged.

He said, "Alright, maybe you have a point. But if you think that's going to stop me from ending this my way, you've got to be dumber than you look."

He was shaking his head. "Now shut up; the tunnel's only a few minutes ahead. Let's see them try to fly a helicopter through a mountain." Dakota could feel prickles along her skin. Her breath came in ragged gasps. The talking hadn't gotten them anywhere useful.

Marcus, though, was still speaking. "Hang on, let's try something else. He's got family, right?"

But Dakota murmured, "I think we can try this my way."

Tyler didn't seem to care what she had to say now. This was a man who had already made up his mind, and Dakota also realized this wasn't who she was.

The only way to get on his side was to compliment his murders but Dakota simply couldn't bring herself to continue groveling. It felt oily, unctuous.

Ahead, she spotted a mountain rising against the horizon. She frowned, her fingers tensed.

The killer was no longer paying attention to her. The cop cars were getting too close—he was gripping the gun in his hand now, snarling. "See if I don't," he was muttering. "See if I *don't.*"

It was like watching a petulant child try to bully their way into getting what they wanted.

But Dakota was well past sympathy.

She tried to move her arm

It was only about half strength. Even her torso still felt heavy, the muscles sedated.

But even at half strength, technique helped. She had spent her entire fighting career dealing with people twice as strong as she was. In Coach Little's gym, he had always put her against male fighters. Technique and skill could win out against size if done properly.

And Tyler Moore was hardly an intimidating figure.

She tried to lean forward now.

She had no seat-belt. No restrictions except for the ache and tingle in her muscles and bones.

Marcus was saying something, but she was no longer listening.

Talking had never been her strong suit. She didn't know what to say. But fighting? And everything like it? That was her domain.

And so, with a sudden gasp, she shoved forward.

She wrapped her weakened arm—the same one she'd been using to manipulate the phone—around Tyler's neck; simultaneously, with her other hand, which was also prickling with a strange numbness, she lashed out and grabbed at his arm carrying the gun.

He cursed, but the sound died as her forearm tightened.

Two gunshots. The already broken windshield lost more surface area. Glass was spewed back into the seat by the blast of air; they were still going so fast. The car began to swerve.

Dakota pulled harder, her muscles so very weak. And yet, she had locked in the rear choke. Her forearm beneath his neck, taut, she still wrangled his other hand, desperate. Her fingers gripped at his wrist. She felt the way his tendons tensed. The gun fired again, this time smashing a section of the dashboard.

She could hear loudspeakers blaring from the direction of the cop cars.

But there was nothing they could do for her now.

She kept her grip in place.

He was yelling, trying to shout. But his voice came choked, muffled due to his constricted throat.

"Stop!" Dakota managed to gasp out

Her phone had tumbled from her shoulder, and was now resting between the front seats.

The killer was trying to aim the gun backwards. But she kept her grip on his wrist, directing it away from her.

The woman next to Dakota was screaming. Her voice sounded weak as well.

The killer dropped the gun. And went for the thermos on the seat.

Dakota gritted her teeth. She tried to move with him. But though she was trained, she was also drugged.

He managed to grab the thermos.

He began to twist at it with the fingers on his right hand. Her muscles tensed as she continued to choke him with her other arm.

And like this, they struggled.

He kept trying to jerk away. He was slowly losing strength to the throttling.

But he fought like a demon; he snarled, trying to bite her. It dappled her skin with spit as the thermos was knocked free into the seat again. He tried to grab it once more. She jerked him back further.

Partly, to choke, but also to try and slow them down. With his body angled back, it wasn't as easy to put full pressure on the gas pedal, but they were still going too fast.

He let out a growl like some sort of animal. And then, as her grip tightened, strength slowly returning, he jerked the steering wheel, hard, and the car screeched, the wind still howling through the windshield, pieces of glass scattering across the ground and the seat. Some pieces hit the metal thermos with a sound like wind chimes.

And then, the car skidded off the road, into the desert through scraggy underbrush. The wheels bounced twice. The bumper hit something, tore through. Vegetation, branches shattered. And then the car flipped, and Dakota shouted in horror.

CHAPTER THIRTY ONE

Dakota blinked, groaning, blood trickling down the side of her face—she couldn't move at first. It took her a second to realize she was now upside down in the car; she hadn't been wearing a seatbelt, but the cushioned headrest and chair in front of her head had absorbed some of the impact. Still, her body felt as if it had been put through twelve rounds with a heavyweight boxer—everything was bruised. She groaned in pain, pushing out of the car, gasping.

She emerged to find herself in the bright glow of a helicopter spotlight. Dakota groaned, sliding along what felt like the roof of the car. Glass scraped beneath her and she winced, gingerly trying to prop herself up but her wrist protested in pain.

She swallowed, and released a shaking breath as she pushed fully out of the vehicle.

She rose slowly, amidst a tangle of brush; spiky leaves and branches grabbed at her shirt. She glanced back towards the car.

A faint voice was emitting a soft moaning sound. But it wasn't coming from the car.

She glanced up and to the side, and realized the would-be victim had landed in the underbrush.

She was still moving. But her leg looked broken.

Her arms were crooked, braced against the tangled branches.

And there, like a shadow against sand, she spotted the killer. He lay on the ground, motionless, his face buried in the earth. His hands spread in front as if reaching for something.

She shook her head, but then stopped the motion, wincing again at the pain in her neck.

"Over here," she tried to call. But her voice was hoarse. The bright beam of the helicopter continued to illuminate her spot. The sirens were wailing from behind her, along the road. She heard the sound of footsteps, shouting.

"Over here!" she said, louder. Her voice strained. She tried to wave, but her fingers ached. She looked down and spotted a shard of glass buried in her palm.

She reached out, and carefully pulled the glass free.

She shot another look towards killer; he wasn't moving.

She wasn't sure that he would move again. Then she turned her attention towards the woman in the underbrush. "Hang tight," she said, wincing. "Help is on the way."

And then she collapsed to the ground next to the car. Her head spinning, blood still spilling down her cheek; she tried to speak, but dark spots danced across her vision and then darkness came in.

***

Agent Marcus Clement hit the pavement in a rush, his heart pounding horribly. The paramedics had arrived now as well, but his eyes were fixed on the bright beam of light cast by the helicopter above. He swallowed, his throat tense as he picked up the pace, hastening forward. He spotted a figure being carried out on a stretcher and his heart jolted.

He rushed forward, one hand extended. He didn't stop to speak, grabbing at the edge of a cloth over the figure's face.

"Hey!" one of the paramedics protested. A cop moved to intervene, but Clement yanked his arm away along with the edge of the sheet.

He stared, but let out a gasp of relief. It wasn't Dakota. Rather, he was staring at a young man with pockmarked skin and dirty blonde hair over a round face. The figure wasn't moving. As the relief cycled through him, he simultaneously felt a jarring lance of guilt. He offered up a small prayer of mercy for the figure on the cot, and then pushed past the officer trying to intervene. "Agent Clement," Marcus snapped. "Where's Dakota? Agent Steele, where is she?"

The officer hesitated, frowning, but Marcus didn't have the patience to show his ID. So instead, he just marched away, long strides moving in the direction of most of the parked vehicles which occupied a large portion of the desert highway. The road had been closed on either end. He'd been forced to park further back, along the shoulder with other emergency vehicles.

Now, as he hastened forward, his gaze landed on a second ambulance. This time, he spotted paramedics tending to someone in the back. He hurried over, breaking into a jog, his heart pounding.

He'd been so far away when she'd found danger. Why had he let her go off on her own?

"Stupid," he snarled beneath his breath. "You're so stupid, Clement." He slapped at his leg, shaking his head in fury as he avoided another stretcher, this time with a woman he didn't recognize. She was sitting up, but her face looked pale and gaunt.

Now, as he neared the back of the ambulance, two more officers stepped forward, holding out hands.

"Excuse me!" one of them said, palm outward.

Marcus tried to keep his tone polite, but he felt something like a grizzly bear restraining itself. "Move your hand," he snapped, his voice shaking.

The officer hesitated. The other met Marcus's gaze.

"Sir," the second officer said, slowly, "Who are you?"

Marcus ripped his ID out, jammed it into the officer's chest then didn't even wait to take it back. Leaving his ID in the cop's grip, Marcus shouldered between the two of them and reached the back of the ambulance.

He felt a jolt of terror.

Dakota Steele lay in the back of the ambulance, eyes closed, cuts and bruises up and down her body. Her turtleneck shirt had been removed, revealing sleeve tattoos and others along her stomach. Two paramedics were hastily bandaging or dabbing disinfectant—judging by the sharp odor—on every exposed area they could find.

It took him a second to realize she was breathing. People didn't tend to the wounds of a corpse.

His horror at the state of his partner was replaced a second later by a dawning sense of greater relief. He leaned forward, one hand braced against the open ambulance doors. "Is she going to be okay?" he insisted, glancing between the two paramedics. "Is she going to be alright?"

The figures in the back of the ambulance shot him a look. One of them, a woman who looked far too young to be trusted with the well-being of his partner, was frowning. "Excuse me, sir, but could you step back please?"

Dakota's eyelashes fluttered briefly. Even unconscious, she still had a solemn, serious expression. It was a rare thing to see his partner's smile. He wished this wasn't the case.

But now, his own features were struggling to arrange themselves.

Part of him wanted to cry. But he held back the emotion. Another part of him wanted to break things. The benefit of being well over six feet with muscles as large as most linebackers was that he was often able to exert himself physically to take out unwanted emotions.

But now, he could feel his stomach twisting, and he shoved away from the ambulance, taking a step back to stare into the compartment.

He could feel his scowl twisting his features. He'd been absent.

He should have been here.

But he'd been an hour away.

"Sir," the woman in the ambulance said, "Please, we'll let you know where we're taking your girlfriend. But you can't be here."

Marcus blinked, shaking his head. "N-no," he said his mouth feeling numb. "No, she's not my..."

He trailed off, shaking his head. He turned, running a hand through his short-cut, neat hair. His fingers were prickling now too as the blood rushed through his system, carrying more than the usual amount of adrenaline.

He shot another quick glance back into the ambulance, scowling.

"Is there anything I can do to—"

"Nothing! Please!" Then, the other paramedic, a surly-faced older man, reached out and slammed the doors shut in Marcus's face.

Clement glared, resisting the urge to reach up and rip the doors back open.

He cursed beneath his breath, a rarity for him, and turned on his heel, staring towards the two cops who were watching him closely. One of them held out Marcus's FBI ID. Clement grabbed this and pointed at the ambulance with the leather sheath. "Where are they taking her? Which hospital?"

"St. Andrew's," the man replied reflexively. He frowned. "We have a chemical weapon on site, sir. We're trying to keep as many people clear as possible. Maybe you should go back to your car..."

Marcus frowned. "What sort of chemical weapon?"

"Still determining," the second officer replied in a rasping, thick voice. "The suspect bragged about its capabilities, but I've been hearing," his fingers tapped against his radio, "it's some sort of gas weapon." He shook his head. "I'm sure we'll know more... *later.*" He emphasized this last word as if expecting Marcus to take some hint.

Clement frowned. *St. Andrew's,* he thought to himself, nodding once. Then, he shot another scathing look towards the license plate of the ambulance, searing it into memory.

He turned, moving rapidly back in the direction of his own vehicle. He'd follow the ambulance to the hospital. Every few steps, he shot a look back, keeping track of the vehicle. He refused to let it out of his sight. If he had to ram one of the damn barricades, he'd do it.

Now, he moved hastily, wanting to reposition his vehicle in case the ambulance set out before he was ready.

As he walked through the procession of emergency vehicles and first-responders, he shook his head in irritation.

Girlfriend... It was obvious they were *partners,* wasn't it? Why on

Earth was the paramedic's instinct *girlfriend*. Marcus shook his head, trying to calm his racing emotions.

It wasn't like that with Dakota. She was his best friend. His partner. They'd worked together for nearly a decade.

And then she'd left...

He swallowed at the memory.

He'd gone and brought her back. He'd needed her help on a case. The other partners they'd tried to pair him with simply weren't as competent. Weren't up to the task...

But... also...

He frowned, remembering the pain it had caused when Dakota had simply quit.

He shook his head in frustration, moving back towards his parked car. It was hard to lose a best friend. A partner. He nodded as he reached his vehicle. The lights flashed as he clicked the locks. A couple of officers looked sharply over, hands on their holsters.

Marcus stiffened, holding up his keys to put them at ease.

Once the cops had relaxed, scowling, Clement shot another look in the direction of the parked ambulance, but then slipped into the front of his own vehicle, still frowning. It had been a long time since he'd felt this strongly about something.

She'd nearly died. When he'd received the call that his partner was driven off the road, he'd nearly rear-ended a semi-truck trying to speed through traffic.

Dakota had nearly died, and he'd been nowhere near.

He snarled, swearing to himself that would never happen again. He refused to let his partner put herself in harm's way without him by her side.

But even as he made this silent oath, he leaned back, his large shoulders sagging against the seat. His head reclined against the cushioned headrest, and he let loose a long, shaking breath.

He knew better than to make an oath he couldn't keep.

That was the problem with Dakota Steele.

No matter how much he wanted to keep her safe...

She just had a knack for putting herself in danger.

Ahead, he spotted red lights flare. The ambulance was moving.

Marcus pulled onto the asphalt road in the heart of the Arizona desert. He pulled out, moving slowly at first, avoiding the officers, but his eyes never left the ambulance carrying his partner.

CHAPTER THIRTY TWO

Dakota picked at the IV drip in her arm, wrinkling her nose at the way the tape adhesive shifted at her prodding. She could feel the needle buried in her skin, though it barely hurt now.

She shifted slowly, wincing with every motion where she propped against the hospital cushion. She let out a faint fluttering sigh, exhaling.

It wasn't *so* bad, she thought.

She'd suffered similar beatings back in her fight career. Though, granted, none *this* bad.

For three days now, they'd kept her at *St. Andrew's,* forcing her to stay in bed. She was getting sick of it. By now, some of the cuts no longer throbbed. The bruises still ached, and a couple of her fingers were cracked and now in a splint on her right hand.

She glanced down to the splinted fingers, wrinkling her nose. These would heal soon enough, according to the doctor. Besides, she'd never been much of a shooter anyway. A few rounds at the firing range and she felt confident she'd correct her aim.

She'd been given thirty stitches, according to one of the doctors. Mostly for some of the cuts on her arms. One particularly bad cut in her palm had required ten stitches on its own.

The IV was replenishing fluids. She'd refused pain medication.

Dakota could feel every jolt, every lance, every ache. But pain medication was off the table. As much as she wanted a drink, as much as she desired some chemical alleviation, she refused to give into this instinct.

She faintly sighed, still leaning against the hospital bed and closing her eyes briefly against a faint headache. It hurt to breath. Hurt to think. But in a way... she was glad.

She hadn't had a drink in five weeks now.

That was the longest she'd gone in years with perfect sobriety.

She smiled slowly, though even this hurt thanks to a cracked lip. But she couldn't help herself. Sometimes, the acute nature of pain was a gift that helped narrow one's focus. And now her focus was narrowed.

She felt a distinct surge of gratitude. Not just for life... but for a life *without* much pain. It was strange to think. But she remembered back in her fighting days how often she'd remembered what it was to have a healthy, working body. Even when something had been broken, or something twisted and placed in a cast or splint, she'd focused on the *rest* of her body. Focused on the way her arms didn't ache if a toe was broken, or focused on just how easily she could breathe if her nose was bashed.

It had helped her cope with the pain, with the damage.

A little bit of gratitude went a long way according to Coach Little. The wonder of eyesight, of taste, of touch, of smell. The wonder of people, of blood vessels, of the breaths she took, of the faint comfort of a breeze. It was all taken for granted.

Pain was a reminder of blessing. Pain was a reminder of the incredible gift of life...

And yet sometimes it was so damn hard.

Dakota's countenance fell as she frowned at this thought. She swallowed, feeling her throat dry. She shifted again, wincing once more as she moved in the hospital bed.

It was this strange war in her mind. This back and forth between the pain and hope. The gratitude and the resentment. The joy and the trauma.

She thought of her father... her sister... Thought of losing them both in different ways.

She thought of her MMA career. And now her FBI career. She thought of all the people who'd never made at it as far. Of the people who'd made it further.

Sometimes, staring at a stalk of grass for long enough, she couldn't help but marvel at the beauty and wonder of the world.

And other times, even surrounded by luxury, she couldn't help but fall into a pit of despair.

It was in *those* times, surrounded by pain, when she practiced gratitude the hardest. Her mind flitted back to something an AA coach had said on their last case...

Sometimes... the person she had to forgive to move on, was herself.

Dakota sighed, reaching up with her tender fingers and brushing at a prickle along her face. She heard a faint sigh, and shot a quick glance into the corner of the room.

Some of the thoughts flitted away. Her mind was able to focus now.

And there, leaning back in one of the uncomfortable visitor chairs, was another reason to be grateful. Agent Marcus Clement had spread his gigantic form across three chairs, his head resting against the wall. His long left arm dangled to the floor where he had made his makeshift cot. He faintly snored as he shifted.

She grinned, watching her partner, but just as quickly hid the smile.

Appearances mattered, after all, and she didn't want to look like some idiot schoolgirl grinning at a sleeping man.

Her partner had been at the hospital from the day she'd woken. For three days now, he'd been there. She wasn't sure what strings he'd been forced to pull with Supervising Agent Carter, but she knew Marcus was in the good graces of their boss anyway.

Still, as she watched her partner, she couldn't help but feel a rising warmth. She'd missed Marcus most of all. Catching the bad guys was a rush. It filled a void.

But doing it alongside her best friend of ten years?

This was one of the greatest gifts life had offered her.

She still couldn't believe she'd up and quit all those months ago. As she studied her partner's sleeping face, she heard a faint buzzing sound.

Dakota glanced over, and noticed her phone lighting up on the bedside table.

She reached out, snatching it, and lifting it, frowning. She'd recognized the name even from where she'd been lying.

Supervising Agent Carter.

Dakota swallowed nervously, picturing the severe expression of the older, safety-conscious woman. The boss wasn't usually in the habit of contacting Dakota personally unless it was to chew her out for some mistake.

Now, Dakota felt a jolt of anxiety as she stared at the phone.

She swallowed faintly, but then, with resigned sigh, she answered.

"Agent Steele," she said, her voice rasping as she did. She hadn't used her words much in the last three days. In a way, it had felt like a verbal holiday.

"Dakota?" said Carter.

This was new, using Dakota's first name without any acerbity. "Yes, ma'am?" Dakota said.

A long breathy pause. For a moment, Dakota thought they'd been disconnected. She glanced at the phone, but the digital timer was still ticking by. She swallowed, and lifted the device again, waiting patiently.

A long sigh then, and Carter said, in her usual crisp, curt tone. "Good job on this last case, Steele. Well done."

Dakota blinked. This was not what she'd been expecting.

Carter sighed once more. It almost sounded like she was trying to hold back what she *really* wanted to say. But then, she continued, "I've reviewed your request for information pertaining to the cold case from twenty years ago... That information is being sent to you as we speak."

Dakota felt another jolt. She froze, wincing, wondering if somehow this was a dream.

"As for the serial case four months ago..." Carter hesitated. There was something strange in the woman's voice. She said, slowly, "I'm not usually in the habit of giving second chances, Agent Steele, I hope you understand this."

"Yes, ma'am," Dakota replied, her voice still rasping.

"In the field, oftentimes a second chance means another dead agent. In the service, my military days, second chances meant dead soldiers. Is that clear?"

Dakota let out a faint puff of air. She hadn't realized Carter had a military background. She wondered which branch, but decided now wasn't the best time to inquire.

"However," Carter said firmly.

Dakota felt a prickle along her spine.

"I'm also not in the habit of being blackmailed."

Dakota hesitated. "Excuse me?"

Carter made a sucking sound. "The more someone doesn't want me to kick over a stone, the more likely I am to topple the damn thing. Does that make sense to you, Agent Steele?"

Dakota felt like she was missing something, but at this point she didn't want to derail the direction of the conversation, so she simply said, "Yes, ma'am."

"Good. In that case, I've also approved your requisition for the information of the case from four months ago. Especially the redacted files."

Dakota hesitated. "Redacted, ma'am?"

"Let's just say... there were parallel investigations. Not *all* of the information was shared. Some might suggest that made it difficult for you to do your job." Agent Carter gave another long sigh. "Now, do you have any questions, Dakota?"

"Umm... Did... did something happen, ma'am?"

"If it did, I wouldn't tell you, would I? Remember your place, Steele. I still don't approve of second chances. But..." her tone softened once more. "You did a good job this time. Foolish, but good. I remember what it is to make choices that risk life and limb for the mission. It's been a few decades, but I remember my youth. Well done, Dakota."

And then the supervising agent hung up.

Dakota's phone buzzed a few times though, notifying her that her private, encrypted email had received new correspondence.

She shifted uncomfortably, staring at her phone. And then, with a rising sense of anticipation, she scrolled to her email. She entered the password, confirmed with the two-factor on her phone, and then scrolled the messages in her inbox.

She ignored a few of the office emails and non-pertinent messages.

But there, at the top, she spotted headings that started with *CLASSIFIED.*

She felt a flicker of excitement. She read the case numbers and her finger hovered. One of the cases was from twenty years ago, involving her missing sister.

The other case from four months ago, which had led to Dakota quitting the BAU and heading home.

She hesitated, gripping her phone.

Sitting there, frowning, she remembered her old supervising agent. Agent Drafuss had left a strange voicemail on her phone. Essentially demanding she leave the case alone.

She'd wondered why the files had been encrypted, why they'd been obfuscated.

And now, according to Carter, there was redacted information she'd never been privy to?

Dakota frowned and her finger settled on the case file pertaining to The Watcher. The notorious serial killer who'd hunted young women. The killer's name had come from the third eye he'd painted in blood on his victims' foreheads.

She shivered in disgust and revulsion, remembering the handiwork of the bastard. He'd never been caught. This, in part, she'd known was her fault.

But now as she clicked the file, her eyes scanned the initial reference page. Familiar memories came flitting back. She studied the information, her throat tight. She could feel an odd knot of anxiety forming in her gut now as she read and re-read the information.

Her skin prickled, and some of the aches and cuts along her arms were forgotten as she leaned forward, the bed creaking somewhat, her foot striking against a thick, plastic barrier at the base of the bed.

But she ignored this, still reading.

Most of the files were familiar. Half of them she'd reported herself. Others she recognized as Clement's. He often used emoticons in his reports. He'd hated doing them by hand. Now, though as she scanned through, she paused, frowning.

Another tab at the top of the sheet simply read: *secondary investigation.*

She wrinkled her nose. What secondary investigation?

Marcus and Dakota had been the only ones assigned to The Watcher... At least, as far as she'd known. They'd corresponded with other agents during the hunt, been aided by the BAU, but no other teams had been assigned primary.

So what was...

She clicked the link.

A link that *certainly* hadn't been available the last time they'd gone over the case. She scanned the information quickly, occasionally distracted by Agent Clement's snoring.

As her eyes darted down the electronic document, she paused. It started out routine enough. A secondary investigation on the side. Nothing urgent, nothing important. Just a routine background check. And then, from there, another check. And from there, two agents from another field office had been assigned to speak to a witness.

She shifted uncomfortably tracking the reports, the tabs of information. Everything seemed aboveboard, so why hadn't this line of questioning been shared with Marcus and Dakota?

She continued scrolling through the reports.

But it was as she reached the later files, that she stopped.

Reports were missing.

One moment, two agents named Greer and Lyndon had been following up on a line of questioning with a witness, and the next... the small taskforce had been disbanded. Dakota wrinkled her nose.

She scrolled back, double-checking.

But it was the same as when she'd first scanned through.

Greer and Lyndon had interviewed a witness identified only as *Witness B.* And then, after the interview with Witness B, the reports ended.

Nothing further.

Dakota shook her head, scrolling to the bottom of the page.

And that's when she stiffened, staring.

The reason behind the sudden end to the secondary investigation was there in big, bold print.

Resources reallocated by SA Drafuss.

His signature was on the line in small, cramped handwriting.

Dakota frowned, scrolling further down, but there was nothing more. The reports ended abruptly. There was no transcript for the interview with *Witness B.* No follow up speculation from either Agent Greer or Agent Lyndon.

Dakota shook her head, reading and re-reading. By the third time, though, she slowly lowered her hand, still clutching at her phone.

Something was off.

After spending ten years investigating, doing case-work, there was a rhythm, a routine to these things. But this secondary, redacted file was like a symphony with no climax. A movie with no credits.

Something was *very* off.

She glanced once more to the name signed at the bottom of the file.

SA Drafuss.

Why had he hidden the file? Why had he tried to bury it? Who was *Witness B*?

Drafuss had quit the BAU after the investigation according to some. Others said he was in witness protection.

None of it made much sense, but Dakota could feel a slow prickle of curiosity as she studied the file.

At least she now had a path forward. Witness B... Greer, Lyndon, Drafuss... One of them might be willing to talk.

She'd just have to find the right leverage.

Did she really think, though, somehow FBI agents were involved with The Watcher? Somehow aiding a killer or helping him escape?

She wrinkled her nose, head back on her pillow as she stared at the white ceiling.

Perhaps not... At least, she hoped not. But... something was off. Something fishy. Carter had done a one-eighty and approved the information request. Because of Dakota's performance on this last case?

The killer's intended victim would survive. The chemical compound found had been a failure according to Marcus who'd been keeping tabs the last few days. The chemist-killer hadn't even created a proper poison gas in his thermos. A dud.

He'd failed in his grand plan.

Though, granted, there was nothing particularly grand about it or him. He'd died in the crash... His computers carried enough information on his chemical experiments to confirm he was behind the murders...

And that was the worst part.

He'd chosen the women for nothing more than sheer jealousy. He saw them as usurpers of his rightful position. Academia itself was the threat, according to a few video diary ramblings they'd found behind an encryption shield. Women he'd seen before while stalking various collegiate locations.

Dakota sighed slowly, shaking her head. To top it all off, she'd missed her date with Bonet... if it was even that.

166

She'd have to contact Greer and Lyndon first. She didn't know either agent, but one of them would have to know *something.*

Which left her with the second request for information.

This one even more personal than the first...

She clicked back on her phone and studied the email heading of the second cold case from twenty years ago.

The only other person who had even *more* information on this cold case was her father. She stared at her phone, not opening the file just yet.

The cold case was one thing... But combining it with her father's most recent research?

She might actually be able to find some answers.

Answers to what had happened to Carol all those years ago. Who had taken her baby sister?

Dakota frowned as she thought about it. She bit her lip and then, slowly, lifted her phone.

Instead of clicking the email at first, instead, she placed a call.

A call that had been a long time coming.

CHAPTER THIRTY THREE

Dakota watched the familiar cityscape pass her by as she frowned out of the rear window of the taxi. Rapid City was exactly how she remembered it.

Some places simply didn't change.

Or perhaps it was her perception that remained the same.

Other things, though, changed in stunning fashion.

Her father had sold his home and moved. Coach Little had warned her about this nearly a month ago. It still stung, though, when she'd found out her father had moved nearly a decade ago.

For ten years, he hadn't told his sole living child that he was in a new house.

Still, she weathered the sting of this realization, clearing her throat and murmuring, "I think it's that blue one up ahead."

The taxi driver was struggling to spot the faded house numbers of the old, run-down portion of town. Her father had traded his old home for a much smaller condo with a worn facade and a single-car driveway he shared with his neighbor by the looks of things.

The driver also spotted the white lettering peeling on the front of the condo, and then flashed a thumbs up, pulling to the side of the road.

Dakota pushed out, slowly, feeling a strange nervousness.

She'd already prepaid the driver and didn't even notice as he pulled away, hastening off for his next fare. For her part, she hadn't brought luggage with her. Hadn't even brought a carry-on. She wasn't going to stay long.

She was here for a nod, a greeting, and a folder.

She hadn't opened the file on the cold case yet. She didn't want to open that particular wound without all the information available.

Which meant a final piece was remaining, and it resided behind that faded, blue door on the left side of the duplex.

She swallowed faintly, feeling a familiar prickle along her back that reminded her of more than one slow march up the steps into an octagon before a particularly bloody fight.

She wasn't here for a fight, though. Wasn't here to argue with her father.

She sighed slowly, massaging the bridge of her nose, and then moving slowly up the sidewalk, approaching the front door.

The porch was worn as well, the rail splintering. A newspaper lay discarded on the ground. There was no printed *Welcome* on the mat.

Just a blank, prickling canvas of brown.

Dakota shifted uncomfortably, the floorboards creaking beneath her.

Part of her had wanted to ask Marcus to come with. Another part of her had wanted to stop by at Coach Little's and get his backup. But she'd ended up scheduling a meal with Little at his favorite pizza joint later in the evening.

This portion of the trip... This was all up to her.

She let out a shaking breath, wincing faintly as she did. Her wounds were healing nicely, but her fingers on her right hand were still in a splint. She'd always been ambidextrous though, equally capable with either hand in fighting or shooting.

Now, though the fingers on her right hand were in a splint, the ones on her left were tapping a new tattoo against her thigh. She'd worn a shirt with a particularly tall neck and long sleeves. All of her tattoos—which her father had hated—were hidden. In fact, part of the reason she'd gotten the tattoos as a teenager was *because* her father hated them.

The age old question: Would you rather be feared or loved?

It didn't take into account it wasn't always the answerer's preference which mattered, but rather the availability of the two in others. And love had never been much of an option.

She reached out, slowly, adjusting her posture, and then knocked on the door in three quick reports.

She then stepped back, and stared at the faded frame, the paint peeling along splintered lines. Her father had never been a very ambitious man. Had never cared much for the appearance of his place. At least, not since Carol had vanished.

And now, Dakota frowned, feeling as solemn as ever as if preparing for an open-casket viewing.

The door didn't open.

She frowned, tried again, knocking louder this time. She pressed the bell. Stepped back again.

And once more, she lingered on the porch, shifting uncomfortably from foot to foot. She thought she heard voices from the duplex next door. She heard the neighbors' door open and close.

Behind her, along the sidewalk a couple of teenagers were zipping by on scooters, shooting her curious glances.

She didn't wave, didn't acknowledge them. In a place like this, a city block in her old stomping grounds, it was usually best to just keep your head down and avoid attracting attention.

She shifted again, but still heard no sound of anyone approaching. She leaned forward, pressing her forehead against the glass, trying to peer into her father's place.

She reached for her phone, pulling it out and double-checking the last text message he'd sent.

4pm. My place. Followed by the address. She checked the time on her phone, double-checked the address, then checked the peeling, white letters over the attached mailbox next to the door.

Right time, right place.

But her old man wasn't there.

She sighed in frustration, turning to glance back down the steps towards the street. Then, with a shrug, she reached out and tried the door handle.

Locked.

She rang the bell again and the soft sound of chimes echoed just on the other side of the door. Then, her phone buzzed.

She frowned, glancing down again.

Couldn't make it. Folder under the mat. Good luck.

She stared at the message, feeling a knot form in her stomach.

Couldn't make it.

She re-read that line again, feeling a slow, rising sense of absolute rage. *Couldn't* make *it?* Her old man wasn't here?

She texted back, her fingers flying furiously. *Where are you?*

She didn't even try to soften the demand.

A long gap between her text and his reply, but then, a single word. *Busy.*

She stared at the message, swallowing now. For a moment, she felt a sudden surge of emotion, starting in her stomach and spreading like fire through her chest. She wanted to cry and scream and pound the door all at once. Part of her wanted to kick the window in.

Busy.

Couldn't make it.

After ten years...

"Shit," she murmured beneath her breath. She wanted to scream.

But when had that ever helped with her father? Screaming, begging, bribing, bragging, pleading, achieving. None of it made a difference. Threats, pain, tears... Nothing. She'd tried everything.

Her old man was as emotionally unavailable as if this *had* been open-casket.

Sometimes... sometimes she just wished he'd up and die so she could grieve him properly instead of being forced to hang onto hope that someday, maybe the two of them could...

She trailed off at this train of thought, feeling a sudden surge of guilt. She winced at the way her mind had been directing itself, and shook her head in frustration.

She re-read the message again. No further clarification. No apology. Just, *busy.*

She could feel the prickle of pain beneath her bandages under her sleeves. Could feel the aching in her ribs. The pain in her stomach, spreading now, also brought with it a strange sense of... longing? An urge?

In that moment, she felt a spike of desire like she hadn't in weeks.

For a moment, her mind cycled through all of her favorite watering holes. The cheap liquor stores, the easy store-owners, the ones who didn't make a fuss or give a second glance.

She missed it.

Missed it all.

An angry sob threatened her throat. But again, like always, Dakota inhaled shakily, forcing the emotion back. Appearances mattered.

Emotions didn't help.

She sighed shakily, letting out a long, gusting breath of air.

The urge to drink wasn't gone, though. She knew she needed to talk to someone. To figure this shit out. Coach Little was going to get food with her later tonight... But that might be too late.

She glanced at her phone. Speed dial.

The same number she'd called the last time she'd been in trouble. A voice on the other end. A voice that actually seemed to care about her.

The same person who'd sat in her hospital room for three days, despite the doctors and even security asking him if he was family.

Marcus was her best friend, but also a confidant.

Talking to him didn't feel like talking to other people nearly so much.

She let out a whooshing breath, determining now that she needed to call *someone.* She refused to give in. Not today. Maybe tonight... maybe tomorrow.

Not today.

Her father could vanish off the face of the Earth for all she cared.

But even as this raging thought flashed through her mind, she knew it wasn't fully true.

Feared or loved.

It wasn't her damn choice, was it?

Her father made the choice for her. She'd gone into fighting for similar reasons.

She shook her head, her lips sealed tight now, warring against the attempt of the rising emotions to control her. She bent over, kicking the doormat to the side and spotting a single, thick red folder beneath it.

She bent over, slowly, and picked the thing up.

The binding of the red folder was worn and scarred. Stained with ink and what looked like dried glue in certain places. It was also *very* thick. Nearly twice the width of most books. She hefted the thing, glancing at the two strands of elastic rope securing the corners.

She didn't open it, though.

Not yet.

No... She jammed the folder beneath her arm and turned on her heel, her back to that stupid, blue door.

Busy.

Fine then. Good riddance.

And again, the vengeful, bitter thoughts felt hollow. If she had her way...

But she didn't, did she?

She hadn't had her way in twenty years.

Her father still blamed her for Carol's disappearance. That was probably the reason. He couldn't bear to even look at her.

Dakota felt these small accusations whispering in her mind, nipping at her like paper cuts. She winced with each one, and moved away from the house, down the gray sidewalks, head down, breathing in, out, slowly.

And then, folder tucked under one arm, heart and chest full of painful emotions, she placed her call.

She swallowed as the phone attempted to connect.

She almost didn't let the call complete. Part of her felt an irrational jolt of terror.

What if *he* didn't answer either?

Then she'd be the single loneliest person in the world, wouldn't she?

Walking away from that door, she wasn't sure she could take it if she was sent to voicemail. Wasn't sure if—

"Dakota?" on the second ring.

"H-hi," she said, slowly, her voice hoarse.

"Hey," Marcus said, cheerful as ever. "How's it going in Rapid City?"

She swallowed, still moving slowly along the gray pavement, doing her best to avoid cracks in the ground. "I..." she trailed off, biting her lip. "I just..."

She could practically feel Marcus frown. She knew him well enough to picture his expression even over an audio call. "Is everything alright?"

The question alone felt like a giant finger jabbing a painful sore. She wasn't sure why, but her voice cracked, shaking with emotion. She tried to swallow, to pass it off as a cough. "I... I got the file I came for," she said, swallowing.

Marcus, though, often was the one who could tell what someone was feeling even if they tried to hide it. There was a temporary pause, but then, in as gentle a voice as he'd ever used, the giant of a man said, "Want to talk about it?"

"No," she said. She hadn't meant to sob, but her voice shook regardless.

"Oh, Dakota," Marcus said, in that same gentle voice. "I'm... I'm sorry."

Now came the anger. As predictable as ever. A moment of vulnerability, pity, then a furious reaction against the response. But she wasn't angry at Marcus. Wasn't angry at anyone but... herself? Her father. The last twenty years?

She didn't know where it came from, but one second she'd been biting her tongue, and the next she cursed at the top of her breath, screaming directly into the phone, face down, eyes on the ground. She screamed again, again. Shouting expletives followed by incoherent yells, like a wounded animal struggling to escape a trap.

Once she was done, she found tears in her eyes. She reached up, frowning, wiping at them. Her hand was shaking where it pulled a single tear drop away.

"I'm sorry," she whispered slowly beneath her breath. "I'm so sorry. I—I don't know what..."

"It's fine," Marcus said. His tone didn't change at all. "Do you... wanna come over, watch something? I'm going through a re-run of one of those funny fauxumentaries."

"I... Come over?"

"Yeah. Tonight. I'm up late anyway. We can watch the show or whatever. I'm kinda bored, if I'm honest. I mean," he added quickly, "you can bring Mark, if you want. Agent Bonet is welcome!"

"Oh... oh, yeah," Dakota said quickly. "Umm, of course." She swallowed. Her voice felt hoarse from the screaming. She felt stupid now, embarrassed.

She tucked the red folder beneath her arm. Then said, "I... I get back in at eight. Is that too late?"

"No, that's perfect." He sounded excited now. "I'll pick you up. I'll order Chinese for three. That work? You can let Mark know, alright?"

Dakota swallowed, exhaling shakily. She wasn't sure why, but that strange emptiness in her chest didn't feel so strong now. "Yeah," she murmured. "Yeah, that's great. Thanks Marcus. Hey... I—I gotta go."

"No prob, see you then!"

Dakota lowered her phone, wiping angrily at her face. She shot a look back towards the small, blue duplex, frowning.

And then, ahead, on the side of the road, she spotted the taxi that had dropped her off. In the front seat, it looked as if the driver was munching on a sandwich.

"Hey!" she called, waving her red folder. "Hey—sir! You still on the clock?"

She broke into a brisk walk, picking up her pace and hastening towards the idling vehicle. Dinner with Little, then a movie night with Marcus.

And Bonet, she reminded herself.

Agent Bonet would want to come too, wouldn't he?

She frowned, shaking her head, and refocusing on the taxi, shifting the folder beneath her arm. On her phone now, and in her hand, she had all the information in the world pertaining to her little sister's disappearance.

But... it could wait.

Yes, she decided.

It could wait until tomorrow.

WITHOUT PITY
Without Pity (A Dakota Steele FBI Suspense Thriller—Book 4)

MMA champ-turned-FBI Special Agent and BAU specialist Dakota Steele is as tough as they come—with brilliance to match, able to catch serial killers no one else can. But when a new victim appears, trapped in an elaborate maze, part of a killer's lair, Dakota realizes she is up against a killer more diabolical than she's ever seen.

"The plot has many twists and turns, but it is the ending, which I did not see coming at all, that totally defines this book as one of the most riveting that I have read in years."
—Reader review for Not Like Us

WITHOUT PITY is book #4 in a new series by critically-acclaimed and #1 bestselling mystery and suspense author Ava Strong.

Still chasing the unsolved murder of her sister, Dakota is burning the candle at both ends, trying to solve the present while trying to fix her past.

Using all the skills at her disposal, Dakota is one step away from entering the killer's mind and decoding his plan.

But will she be fast enough to save another life?

A complex psychological crime thriller full of twists and turns and packed with heart-pounding suspense, the DAKOTA STEELE mystery series will make you fall in love with a brilliant new female protagonist and keep you turning pages late into the night.

Book #5 in the series—WITHOUT HOPE—is now also available.

"This is a chilling, suspenseful page turner that just might leave you scared at night!"
—Reader review for Not Like Us

completely surprised by the ending. I have to say, I am thrilled that this is the first in a series. My only complaint is that the next one isn't out yet. I need it!"
—Reader review for His Other Wife

"An incredible, intense, spellbinding, enjoyable story. It will keep you captivated until the end."
—Reader review for His Other Wife

Ava Strong

Bestselling author Ava Strong is author of the REMI LAURENT mystery series, comprising six books (and counting); of the ILSE BECK mystery series, comprising seven books (and counting); of the STELLA FALL psychological suspense thriller series, comprising six books (and counting); and of the DAKOTA STEELE FBI suspense thriller series, comprising five books (and counting).

An avid reader and lifelong fan of the mystery and thriller genres, Ava loves to hear from you, so please feel free to visit www.avastrongauthor.com to learn more and stay in touch.

BOOKS BY AVA STRONG

REMI LAURENT FBI SUSPENSE THRILLER
THE DEATH CODE (Book #1)
THE MURDER CODE (Book #2)
THE MALICE CODE (Book #3)
THE VENGEANCE CODE (Book #4)
THE DECEPTION CODE (Book #5)
THE SEDUCTION CODE (Book #6)

ILSE BECK FBI SUSPENSE THRILLER
NOT LIKE US (Book #1)
NOT LIKE HE SEEMED (Book #2)
NOT LIKE YESTERDAY (Book #3)
NOT LIKE THIS (Book #4)
NOT LIKE SHE THOUGHT (Book #5)
NOT LIKE BEFORE (Book #6)
NOT LIKE NORMAL (Book #7)

STELLA FALL PSYCHOLOGICAL SUSPENSE THRILLER
HIS OTHER WIFE (Book #1)
HIS OTHER LIE (Book #2)
HIS OTHER SECRET (Book #3)
HIS OTHER MISTRESS (Book #4)
HIS OTHER LIFE (Book #5)
HIS OTHER TRUTH (Book #6)

DAKOTA STEELE FBI SUSPENSE THRILLER
WITHOUT MERCY (Book #1)
WITHOUT REMORSE (Book #2)
WITHOUT A PAST (Book #3)
WITHOUT PITY (Book #4)
WITHOUT HOPE (Book #5)